DUSK SECRETS

ADDISON BECK

Book formatting by Addison Beck

Interior Paperback formatting by Breathless Lit

Cover Design by Ariadna Basulto with Chaotic Creatives

CONTENT AND TRIGGERS

I like my sweet, low-angst, fluffy stories. I just want to make people smile. However, this story came to me, and it's a lot darker than my other works. Please, pay attention to the triggers. Your mental health is the most important.

Severe Homophobia (*Homophobic slurs, the concept that being gay is sinful, lots of talk about people who are gay going to hell*)
Religious Themes (*Mass, prayers, discussions of whether God is real*)
Violence
Profanity
Mentions of Suicide (*A character the MC knew committed suicide years ago off-page*)
Drugs (Weed and Molly)
18+ Sexual scenes
For a more detailed breakdown of triggers and content, please visit my website www.addisonbeckromance.com

PREFACE

Dusk Secrets came to me in a dream.

I had this one perfect scene in my head about a fish going where no fish should go (you'll get to that soon enough) and that was it. I never imagined I'd grow to love Jarred and Noah the way I do. I also never imagined I'd resonate as much with their characters as I have now.

Growing up in a deeply religious Catholic family, I understand the pressure one can get put under when trying to come to terms with their sexuality. Luckily, my family embraced me and continued to love me for who I am, but not everyone has the same experience.

This is also in no way trying to insult or debase the Catholic faith. I am taking no stance on my personal opinions on the Catholic church.

I'd like to make a point and say that not every coming-out story is the same. If you've gone through that experience, you know that they are widely different, and this is just one take on what it would be like for two born-and-raised Catholics to find love in the place they never expected it.

There are a lot of sensitive topics in this story, so please read the trigger warnings if needed. My MCs are not perfect, so don't expect them to be, please. This story will get frustrating at times, so be patient with them. Change doesn't happen overnight.

I hope you enjoy this story and thank you for continuing this journey with me!

For my friends from every corner of the world that kept me going.

For Mads. Thanks for dealing with me. You're truly a breath of fresh fucking air, and I love your face.

CHAPTER 1
JARRED

"I just don't understand why you're doing this!"

I resist the urge to throw my phone against the wall. My frustration is seeping out of me in waves, darkening the bright and shiny mood I woke up in. I swear, it's like pulling teeth with her.

"Jenny, I'm doing this because you *cheated* on me," I try to explain to my soon-to-be ex-wife who doesn't seem to understand that this is going to happen, whether she likes it or not.

It's been three months of this, and the wound is still sore. Three months since I found her in bed in our Asheville apartment with a member of our church. Since then, I've started the process of getting an annulment through the church, but she isn't making it easy. All I want is to wash my hands of her, but she's determined to make our marriage work despite her betrayal.

"I already gave Father Matteo the copy of our baptismal certificates, the church marriage certificate, and the formal annulment petition. The only thing I'm waiting for is for you to sign those fucking divorce papers."

"Jarred Charles Walker! Watch your mouth!" she screeches, and I imagine she's grabbing her imaginary pearls at my language. *"What has gotten into you?"*

I've never in our twenty-five years of marriage cursed at her. It's no wonder she's shocked, but what is she expecting? Is she expecting that I'll forgive her just like she wants? Does she think that I want to be with someone who jumped into bed with another man after more than two decades of being together?

I hate to admit that during our marriage, I had been a doormat. I let her talk to me however she wanted, and I never complained. I set the precedent that she could do and say whatever she wanted to me without repercussions. Even after she cheated on me, we attended marriage counseling through the church with our priest, but I couldn't move past her infidelity. I was okay with her dictating our every choice —where we got married, where we went to church, how we raised our twins—but I draw the line at sleeping with another man.

All I want is for her to sign the divorce papers, so I can get an annulment through the church. The Catholic church believes that marriage is a life-long bond, a sacred pact that's made in the eyes of the Lord that is never meant to be broken. Technically speaking, I can't get married through the church again unless I get this annulment. Now, I don't have any plans to get married again at forty-five years old, but I want to be free and clear of her. In the eyes of the law and the eyes of God.

"You, Jenny. You have gotten into me," I say, gritting my teeth and asking the Lord for restraint so I don't throttle her through the phone. "I'm sorry if I upset you, but we're over. There is no making amends. There is no more marriage counseling with Father Matteo. We've said all we need to say, and I'm ready to move on with my life."

"*But Jarred—*"

"The only thing I want to hear from you is that you're signing the papers and mailing them over. Until then, goodbye, Jenny."

I hang up the phone before I can say the nasty words that are on the tip of my tongue. Today started off as such a good day. Today, the camp counselors finally show up—one week before the camp officially begins—and this is usually one of my favorite days.

I established Camp Trinity twenty years ago and, in twenty years, it's turned into something I can really be proud of. My twins were the inspiration behind setting up Camp Trinity. I wanted to give them a place where they could get in touch with their spirituality and get closer to God. Since then, it's become a place for kids of all ages to come and experience a peaceful and religious environment that helps them strengthen their faith and their character. The twins are now twenty-five and have grown out of the camp age, but I'll always hold the memories of them growing up here close to my heart.

Camp Trinity is hidden in beautiful Mount George, four hours outside of Asheville, and surrounded by nothing but forest and lakes. During the school year, we hold little events—corporate team bonding, church retreats, and day camps—but summer is my favorite time of the year.

I stretch as I get out of bed, my joints popping and aching as I make my way to the dresser. I pull out the nicest Camp Trinity polo I own and a pair of tan slacks. I want to put my best foot forward with the counselors today. I don't want them to see a bitter old man who's going through a messy annulment with his bitch (forgive me, Lord) of a wife. I want them to see someone they can count on, someone they can lean on, someone they can trust to lead them.

I dress quickly and take a look in the mirror when I'm done. I don't *think* I look my age. Sure, my blonde hair has a few streaks of grey and there are little wrinkles around my brown eyes, but apart from that, I seem young enough. I'm only forty-five. I have my whole life ahead of me. But it doesn't seem like that some days. It seems like my life is exactly what it's destined to be.

Lonely and disappointing.

I head to the kitchen and fill up my thermos with the automatic coffee that brewed a few minutes ago, grab my clipboard with the camp counselor information, and head out of the door. The deep breath I take once I leave my cabin does make me feel better. The sun is just starting to rise, so there's a pretty pink hue to the sky as I make my way to the camp entrance that's just a short walk away from my cabin.

I'm happy and rejuvenated when I see that all my camp counselors are already here and waiting for me. It makes me even happier to see the familiar faces who decided to come back for another summer. There are twenty of them in total and most of them have been campers themselves. Their ages range from eighteen to twenty-two years old, and they're from all over the country. They're good Catholic children—

polite and respectful, kind and generous—and everything I want our younger campers to be.

"Good morning!" I say, adding an extra skip to my step as I approach them. All eyes and all smiles get directed my way. I try to match that youthful energy this early in the morning as I stop in front of them. "For those of you who don't know me, I'm Jarred. I'm the director here at Camp Trinity. I want to say how happy I am that all of you have decided to come and join us this summer. For my returners, I want to welcome you back. I expect that this summer is going to be the best we've ever had!"

Sure, that might seem like an exaggeration, but I mean it. It's the twentieth anniversary of the camp and I want it to be the greatest season. If anything, I *need* it to be. With my upcoming divorce and the prospect of an entirely different life, I want this one constant to remain special to me. When all the counselors start applauding, I have a feeling that my wish is going to be granted.

"Thank you! Settle down, settle down!" I yell, my voice drowned out by their applause and cheers. "Okay, so those of you who have been here before know the drill. I'll start off by calling roll, we'll get you sorted into your bunks, and then we'll have a tour of the camp. Your assigned positions will be given later after you all fill out the sign-up sheet."

"Mr. Walker!"

"Kendall, I've told you to call me Jarred for the last four summers," I joke, turning to the overly caffeinated, overly preppy girl with the dirty-blond pigtails whom I've known since she was ten. "What is it?"

She smiles brightly as she takes a step forward. "When are you going to choose bunk leaders?"

Kendall, ever the perfectionist, has been a bunk leader for the last two years. It's a simple job. With around a hundred kids to watch over, I can't be expected to supervise all the counselors as well. Bunk leaders are in charge of around five camp counselors, and they report directly to me with any questions or concerns.

Kendall has been a good bunk leader, so I smile tenderly at her youthful optimism as I address her. "Thank you for reminding me. I'll appoint the bunk leaders at the end of the week before the campers get here. Any other questions?"

In a slightly creepy manner, the hoard of counselors all simultaneously shake their heads. I take a quick sip of my coffee before I start calling roll. With every name I pass, I feel more and more confident that I've selected a good group of young adults to represent the camp. I have the returners I trust the most—Kendall, Patrick, Sheridan, Bryce—and a few promising newcomers that I picked out of dozens of applicants.

"Noah Scott?" When I don't hear an immediate response, I glance up from my list and furrow my brows. "Noah?"

"I'm right here."

I don't think I'm entirely prepared when Noah steps out from behind the crowd of counselors to show himself.

Now, I'm not a judgmental man—the right is reserved solely for God—but Noah doesn't *look* like our typical counselor. Where everyone else is very clean-cut, he's all grunge with his shaggy black hair hidden under a metal band beanie and his black-ripped jeans that seem two holes close to tearing apart. His face is filled with piercings—his eyebrows, his bottom lip, and two on his nose—and as he shuffles from one foot to the other while picking at the black nail polish on his fingers, I'm left wondering if there's been some mistake in the registration.

When he brushes his long bangs out of his face, I'm greeted by a pair of angry hazel eyes. There's something resembling hatred in them, of what, I don't know. But what I do know is that something stirs in my gut as I look into those hateful eyes.

Something that I long thought I had buried.

Something that I've spent years praying away.

Something shameful and blasphemous.

Lust.

Crap.

CHAPTER 2
NOAH

I can't believe I actually have to go to summer camp like I'm twelve.

Well, technically I'm a counselor, but still.

This is the exact opposite of what I planned on doing for the entire summer. I'm nineteen. I should be spending the summer dicking around with my friends and traveling. I should be going to parties and having a great time, but instead, I'm here.

Three months. I have to spend three months in this hellhole surrounded by people who look and act nothing like me.

Fuck my parents. They had freaked out when their clean-cut, perfectly pressed, Catholic son had come back during winter break with piercings, dyed black hair, and lime-green nail polish. It had been their idea and their demand that I work at Camp Trinity. Apparently, the University of North Carolina has been corrupting my good Catholic upbringing, and I needed to go to a place where I could be reminded of my connection with God.

What a fucking joke.

When they showed me the application they sent to Camp Trinity on my behalf, I was ready to tell them to fuck off. I wasn't going to go to a Catholic summer camp in the middle of nowhere-North-Carolina. I wasn't going to surround myself with hundreds of fucking kids or a bunch of religious zealots. But when they threatened to stop paying for my college, I caved. The deal is that I spend one summer at a Catholic camp, and they'll continue to pay for my remaining three years at UNC.

As the rest of the counselors and I walk through the campgrounds to our bunks, I'm starting to think that this will be harder than I thought. I pull my cell phone out of my pocket and cringe when I see that there's zero reception. That means I'm stuck here without any contact with the outside world. Thank fuck I brought enough weed to last me through the summer.

"Here they are!" Jarred booms, his loud voice echoing through the forest as he gestures at the four cabins in front of us. "Home sweet home for the next three months!"

Yeah, home sweet *fucking* home.

I curl my upper lip in disgust as he leads us into one of the cabins. This place is ancient. The wood is all damp and moldy, the ceilings cannot be structurally sound, and—

Are those fucking *bunk beds*?

Jarred must see the look on my face, and I swear he fucking blushes as he scratches the back of his neck. The other campers are mulling around, wandering through each bunk to take a look inside when he approaches me. "I know it's not much, but our fundraiser this year should get us enough money for a renovation in the winter."

"It's…" I trail off because I don't want to lie, but I also don't want to offend him within the first hour of meeting him. "Nice."

His responding white smile is enough to knock me on my ass.

Jarred Walker is an attractive man. He's got these mocha brown eyes that perfectly complement his salt-and-pepper blond hair. He's not overtly muscular under that dad polo he's sporting, but he fills it out nicely. I can also admit that I checked out his ass on the way here—by accident of course—and those cheeks are no joke.

It was two weeks into my freshman year at UNC that I realized I was bisexual. I was at my first-ever frat party, took some Molly for the first time ever, and made out with a random guy while we dry-humped in the backyard. Growing up a strict Catholic, I never imagined that I would enjoy having a guy shove his tongue down my throat but, that night, my cock wholeheartedly disagreed.

Jarred Walker is far from my normal type, but as he turns around to talk to the other campers, and I get another glimpse of those ass-hugging slacks, I can admit that he's pushing all my buttons.

But I also can't forget that I don't want to be here, and there's no way Mr. Holy-Man himself would appreciate me checking him out. I like to mess around, but I'm not a pervert.

"Noah, Bryce, Patrick, and Joshua, you'll be staying here," Jarred says, that adorably wide smile still on his face. Fuck, how can someone be so filled with energy at five in the fucking morning?

"Looks like we're bunkmates," the red-haired guy tells me, grinning as he walks over to the first set of bunk beds by the door. "Do you want to be the top or bottom?"

I snort at the crude joke I make inside my head as Jarred walks out with the rest of the counselors to show them where they're staying. I dump my duffel bag on the ground beside the bed. "I'll bottom any day."

I should have known better than to expect some sort of laugh from him. I guess I've been away from Catholic kids for a while and must have forgotten that the Holy Spirit doesn't have a sense of humor.

He doesn't even blink as he extends his hand out warmly. "That's fine with me. I'm Patrick, by the way. Noah, right?"

"Yup," I say, popping the 'p' as I plop down on the bed.

"Where are you from?"

"Just outside of Asheville, but I go to UNC."

"Oh, awesome! I go to Belmont Abbey!"

Great. Belmont Abbey is the only Catholic university in North Carolina. Just my luck that I get roomed with a bunch of guys not even remotely similar to me. Not that I was really expecting any better.

"Hey, Patrick? He doesn't give a fuck," Bryce—I think—says, slapping the back of Patrick's head.

Joshua grabs his crotch crudely, sneering at Patrick. "Why don't you just go ahead and suck his dick if you're such fast friends?"

Okay. I don't like these guys. Just because I was feeling iffy about Patrick, doesn't mean I was going to be a grade-A dick to him. Bryce and Joshua stand in front of me—perfectly pressed khakis in place—and I can already tell this is going to be a long summer. I know guys like them. They think that just because they have daddy's money, they can do whatever the fuck they want.

They're going to learn real quick that I don't fuck with that.

I square up to Bryce, puffing my chest out as I approach him. "Do that again and see what happens."

Bryce's brows shoot up to his hairline as he looks between me and a nervous Patrick. It seems like he didn't expect me to do anything about the fact that he practically hit another counselor. He curls his lips in a cruel smirk as he backs up with both his hands in the air. "Fine, I'll leave you two pussies to it."

I roll my eyes at his halfhearted attempt at an insult. The word rolls right off my back. I know better than to get flustered and hurt by a jackass like him. But when I look at Patrick, I do feel bad. His cheeks are all flushed and his eyes dart nervously behind his glasses as he watches Bryce and Joshua walk out of the cabin.

"Hey," I say, resting my hand on his small shoulder. "Don't listen to that shit. They're just trying to rile you up. If you let them, they win."

He blushes as he nods. "I know. Thank you for stepping in the way you did."

"No problem. Has it always been like that?"

"At least for the past three summers," he says with a sad shrug, looking down like he's far too interested in his shoes. "We used to be friends when we went here together as kids."

I frown and squeeze his shoulder. "That sucks, man. Just don't let it get to you."

"I won't," he says, but I have a feeling it hits him deeper than he's letting on. "We should really go meet them outside for the tour. Mr. Walker doesn't like us being late."

"You mean *Jarred*?" Because there's no way in hell I'm calling him Mr. Walker. "He seems like a stick in the mud."

"No, he's like super cool," Patrick says, waving his hands widely in the air. "He's the best."

"Okay then." I roll my eyes, not quite ready to base my opinion of Jarred on my uber-religious bunkmate's assessment. I stand up, tossing my beanie and ruffling my hair as I head to the door. "Let's go then."

When we get outside, Jarred and the rest of the counselors are all waiting for us, and I don't miss the dirty looks Bryce and Joshua send my way. They can go fuck off. I've witnessed firsthand what bullying can do to someone, and I'm not about to let them push Patrick around regardless of the fact that he's old enough to take care of himself.

"Are we ready for the tour?" Jarred asks us with nothing but politeness in his voice.

Patrick gives him an enthusiastic nod while I give him a curt dip of my head. Jarred starts off by explaining that our cabins are our homes for the next three months and that we need to keep them clean and in pristine condition while here. He goes through the mandatory list of rules—no smoking, no drinking, no messing around—and I make it a point to add those things to my own personal bucket list for the summer.

He shows us where the showers are—boys and girls separate, of course—and a little hangout area solely reserved for the counselors. Then there's the mess hall, the art studio, the music room, the outdoor sports hut, and finally, the chapel.

"Most of you already know this, but I'll go through our schedule again for our newest members," Jarred says, opening the door for us as we all pile into the building. "We'll have weekly mass here held by Father Matteo and daily ministry groups led by you."

I stop at that. *Ministry groups.* He's telling me that I have to lead a group of kids in prayer and talk about the righteousness of God. I don't have the fondest memories of youth groups growing up. It was all prayer and a bunch of adults shoving their beliefs down our throats. It always felt so suffocating, so hypocritical, and so pointless. Now I guess I'm in charge of all that suffocating, hypocritical, pointless bullshit.

Fuck me. This is going to be a long ass summer.

CHAPTER 3
NOAH

Once the tour is all done, Jarred takes us to the mess hall to sign up for the activities we want to be in charge of once the campers get here.

The list is long and detailed, no doubt a perfect representation of what goes on inside that man's head, and there are too many options to choose from. Too many options that I don't give a flying fuck about. There are jobs listed for guitar lessons, dance classes, arts and crafts, hiking, van duty, kitchen cleanup, and so many more that seem unreasonable for twenty counselors to take care of.

I bite the tip of the pen between my teeth as I take a look at the list, contemplating whether I'd like to get my ears shattered by a group of elementary schoolers playing the guitar or get eaten by a bear when I inevitably get lost leading a hike.

"What are you going to choose?"

I look up at Jarred who's torn himself away from the other counselors getting breakfast to come and talk to me. He keeps his distance, hands clasped behind his back as he looks down at the paper.

"Um, art, I guess?" I sign my name next to the painting slot. Art is something I've always been into, and if I have to teach a group of kids anything, it'll be how to draw a reasonably decent sunset.

He raises a brow. "Just that?"

"Well, what else do I need?"

"Everyone has to do van duty once a week, so you have to put your name next to a slot. You also alternate which days you'll be a lifeguard at the lake. Did you get your lifeguard training done before you came here?"

My face heats in embarrassment. I was supposed to do that? "No."

His smile is sympathetic as he looks down at me. "It's okay. I'm certified to teach you, so we'll get that sorted up before the kids get here next week."

"Anything else?" I say, and I find it hard to keep the bite out of my voice at his condescending tone.

His eyes widen a tad at my words. He takes a step closer and leans over my shoulder to point at the last page on the table. "You have to sign up for when you're going to lead the ministry groups."

I know I should be focusing on some sort of witty comeback, but I can't when he's this close to me. He smells like something citrusy mixed with sandalwood, and it's entirely too appealing. He's so close I can feel his breath next to my ear, and I curse myself for how long it's been since I've come because my dick is starting to get interested. I take a quick step away from him.

"Right," I say, scribbling my name on a random date on the paper. "Will do. Thanks, Jarred."

"If there's anything else you need, let me know." He clears his throat, an unusual flush creeping up his tan neck as he nods. "Team bonding starts in twenty minutes."

My face pales as he walks away. First, there was youth ministry and now there's team bonding? Fuck, I really do hate my parents.

I finish up with the signup sheet, barely registering the rest of the blanks I'm filling, and head to the food line. For a camp, this place actually has a decent selection. I take a couple of scoops of eggs and three slices of bacon and make my way to the tables. I automatically bypass where Bryce and Joshua are sitting with some other counselors and plop myself down at the table where Patrick sits with a pretty girl in pigtails.

"Hi, Noah!" the girl beams, extending her pretty manicured hand out to me. "I'm Kendall."

"Good to meet you," I grunt, accepting her hand. She looks just like the girls I went to high school with. Perfect Catholic girls with sweet smiles and crosses dangling from their necks. She looks nice enough, and Patrick definitely doesn't mind her based on the way he's practically drooling next to her. I gesture at their untouched plates. "Aren't you going to eat?"

A look of mortification pops up on Kendall's face as I dig into my eggs. "Eat? Before giving thanks?"

Right, how could I have forgotten? I guess my parents were right about UNC corrupting me because it entirely slipped my head that—heaven forbid—we eat before saying grace.

I'm fucking starving, so I dig in, not giving a flying fuck that some counselors are looking at me like I'm crazy. Jarred raises one brow at my actions, looking perplexed and...intrigued, but he clears his throat quickly and starts to say grace.

"Bless us, O Lord, and these, Thy gifts which we are about to receive from Thy bounty. Through Christ, our Lord. Amen."

A chorus of 'amens' followed by a dozen signs of the cross follows his words. As we eat, I quietly take in my surroundings. It sucks that the counselors' cabins are in terrible condition, seeing as though the rest of this camp is actually really nice. The mess hall is huge, bright with white walls and exposed wooden beams. There's one huge crucifix at the back of the hall over the food line, and I can count three pictures of the Virgin Mary littering the walls.

I think this is where reality sets in. I really am here. At Catholic church camp. For three months.

I become filled with bitter resentment as I stab at my bacon. I didn't always use to be this anti-religion. I think at one point in my life, I actually liked going to church. It wasn't until my senior year that I started having doubts.

Jacob Cooper was a scrawny kid who went to school with me. I didn't interact with him much besides the odd hello and the times we were paired up in science, but he was a nice enough guy. Apparently, someone had caught him making out with a boy from the next town over, and the rumors had spread like wildfire. He was mercilessly bullied about his sexuality until one day he couldn't do it anymore and killed himself.

We held a vigil for him at the school mass the next day, but when we all went to pray, I couldn't muster up the will. There could have been other demons he was battling with, signs that we all missed, but I could only focus on one thing.

God must not be real and, if he is, he's a fucking bitch.

Why would God do that to him? Why could He just sit idly by and allow a nice kid like Jacob Cooper to suffer so much? For something he had no choice in? How could a real god love followers who inflicted so much pain on someone so innocent?

I think that's when I realized there was no point in believing in someone who's so cruel, so selfish, and so apathetic to the suffering of others. I think that's where it began—not just the dislike—but the *hatred* of Him.

"So, Noah," Kendall starts. "Where are you from?"

I push aside the memory of Jacob Cooper and answer. "A town just outside of Asheville, but I go to UNC."

"That's so cool," she says, green eyes wide and bright. "Are you a freshman?"

"Going into my sophomore year."

"What made you want to join us at Camp Trinity?"

I scoff, uncaring when Kendall's face falls just a tad. "Want? That's a strong word. My parents made me come here before threatening to stop paying for my school."

"Oh, I'm sorry," she says with a flush, ducking her head as she pushes her eggs around with a fork.

I feel bad at the look on her face. So what that I'm in this crappy situation? I shouldn't take it out on her. I sigh and try my best to muster up a smile. "Did I hear Jarred say that this is your fourth summer here?"

This perks her up immediately. She nods eagerly as she gestures at Patrick. "Patrick and I have been coming here since we were kids, and we joined as counselors as soon as we graduated high school."

"I know you're being forced to be here, but you might like it," Patrick says with a shrug. "I know I said it before, but Jarred is really cool. He always tries to make sure his counselors have a good time."

"What's his story?" I ask, my curiosity burning as my eyes wander to Jarred eating at the corner of the room with a group of counselors.

"I shouldn't say," Kendall mutters, sharing a look with Patrick. "It's considered a sin to gossip."

Patrick chokes on his eggs. "Since when?"

"Since forever," she says, chewing on her bottom lip. "Mama told me, but I'm not supposed to say anything. Apparently, Mr. Walker is getting an annulment."

"He is?" Patrick asks, his jaw dropping in shock. "What happened?"

"Mama says he caught his wife cheating on him," Kendall explains before turning back to me. "Personally, I never really cared for Mrs. Walker. She was always just so…mean to him."

"Really?" I question, keeping my eyes on Jarred and feeling fluttering in my chest when he laughs at something one of the girls tells him. "What would she do?"

"She'd always correct him in public," Patrick says. "She'd drop comments about his weight every now and then. One time, she even called him an idiot in front of the congregation."

Now that doesn't sound very Jesus-loving. What a bitch. First of all, there's absolutely nothing wrong with Jarred's weight. He's not completely ripped, but who is? I know I've only known him for a solid two hours but—my resentment aside—he does seem nice. Nobody deserves to be treated like trash by someone they love. I should know. My parents do it enough for me.

I don't know if my thoughts of him have somehow worked their way to his table, but it's at this second that he looks up in my direction. We make eye contact and I have to suppress the shudder that races through me.

No man has ever affected me this way before. He's not even fucking doing anything, just staring at me. Granted, for a very prolonged period of time.

There's something simmering under those brown eyes, something dark and wanting. It catches me off-guard. The happy-go-lucky camp director isn't here anymore. In his place is someone filled with reckless layers and agonizing pain.

But then he looks away and smiles at the girl next to him, and I swear I didn't just make what just happened up. *Something* happened. Something passed between us like a current. Something hot and dangerous and consuming.

And I'll be damned if I'm not going to find out what that *something* was.

CHAPTER 4
JARRED

I'm drenched in sweat.

I don't know why I planned flag football as one of our team-bonding games and, at twice their age, I have no idea why I decided to play with the counselors.

I'm practically limping off the field, resisting the urge to rub at my sore knees as I take a seat on the bench. I grab my sports drink and chug it down in a few gulps, breathing heavily as I watch the counselors continue to play without me.

Against my better judgment, my eyes track Noah as he races across the field, football in hand, looking like he owns the place. At first glance, you wouldn't think someone like him would be good at sports, but he's kicking everyone's butts.

There's the stirring in my gut again. The clenching of my heart. The heating of my skin. Noah's coated in a slick sheen of sweat, his frame gracefully avoiding anyone who tries to get his flag. He's a thing of beauty, a perfect beacon of youth, and I need to tear my eyes away from him before I think of something I'll regret.

This isn't the first time I've thought of a man in…*that* way. Growing up, I always appreciated the attractiveness of my friends, but I've kept it to myself. Those thoughts are sinful, immoral, and *wrong*, and I have never given into temptation. Just to think of it would be an affront to God.

But the way the light bounces off Noah's lip ring makes me think of places I'd like to feel that ring.

I stand quickly, flushed and too hot as I march toward Kendall. She played with the first team and is acting as a cheerleader for both teams now. She might be one of the sweetest and purest people I've ever met.

"Hey, Kendall?"

She turns to me with that trademark wide smile. "Yes, Mr. Walker."

"Jarred," I correct her. "I have to step away for a second. Do you mind monitoring the game for me and rotating the teams when their time is up?"

She beams at me and nods rapidly, and I can only imagine she's overjoyed at the idea of the extra responsibility. "One hundred percent! You can totally count on me!"

"Wonderful," I say sincerely, giving her a quick nod before I start to walk away. "I'll be back in a bit!"

I walk away from the field and fight against the urge to look back at Noah to see if he's scored another point. My feet take the automatic route that's ingrained in their memory. There's only one place I need to be right now and one person I need to see.

As I enter the chapel, I make sure to do the sign of the cross before I step any further. Whenever I'm in here, I always puff out my chest a little. The majority of the money I had when I started Camp Trinity was put right into the construction of this building. It's beautiful, large, with oak pews that stretch twenty rows. I was optimistic when I told the builders how big I wanted it, hoping that the camp would grow to the hundreds rather than the dozens we started with. My hope and faith were rewarded, and now it's standing room only when we conduct mass.

I walk through the pews, making sure to touch each and every one of them as I head to the office in the back. It's the middle of the day, so Father Matteo should be in his office setting up. The door is slightly ajar when I reach it, so I let myself in. As predicted, Father Matteo is unpacking his things and organizing his desk. He's not here all year round but only comes during the summer months.

He doesn't exactly look like your stereotypical priest. Father Matteo is young, in his thirties, I think. He has sleek black hair he keeps neatly done, and there's no trace of any wrinkles or age lines around his face. When most people think of a priest, they think of old saggy men, but Father Matteo looks like he could be on the cover of a magazine.

I clear my throat to get his attention, and his brows dip when he sees me. "Jarred," he says, waving at me as I take a step into his office. "I didn't think I'd see you today. Didn't the new counselors arrive this morning?"

"They did." I gulp, looking nervously around the office as I bounce on my heels.

"You look..." He pauses for a moment, searching for the word. "... flushed. Is there something you need?"

I feel heat shoot up the back of my neck. I probably look like a sweaty mess. I stutter through my words. "I—um—I need to do confession."

He cocks his head to the side, and I'm not sure what he's looking for when he looks at me. It takes him a moment, but he nods. He gestures down at his civilian clothes. "I need to change, but why don't you meet me in the confessional? I'll be there shortly."

I want to tell him to hurry up but that would be rude. Instead, I go to the confessional that sits just outside of his office. I take a deep breath as I enter the booth, and the stifling feeling of guilt hits me like a truck. Even when my sins aren't grave, I always feel like I'm suffocating when I'm in one of these. It's like God is right above me, judging me, and waiting for me to confess all my blasphemous sins. I'm thankful when I hear the door on the other side of the partition open only a few minutes later.

"Forgive me, Father, for I have sinned," I whisper, making another sign of the cross as I clasp my hands out in front of me. "I have committed a grave sin against God, and I seek forgiveness."

"What's the sin you think you've committed?" Father Matteo asks, his deep voice soothing.

"I've had..." I trail off, but I know I need to continue. Father Matteo will understand my wayward thoughts, but they have to stay like that. Just thoughts. As long as I don't act on them, it can't be too bad, right?

"I have been having...inappropriate thoughts about one of our new counselors."

He waits for a beat before he asks his question. "What kind of thoughts, my son?"

"I...I don't want to say," I admit slowly. "Thoughts of their attractiveness, I guess."

"Have these thoughts been sexual in nature?"

"No. Not at all," I insist urgently, but I can feel the lie on my tongue. "But I don't want to stray. I need God to forgive me for this sin I've committed."

"I don't necessarily think it's a sin to find somebody attractive," he says. "Attraction is normal. The counselors are all of age. Would the relationship be inappropriate? For sure. But sinful? Only because you're still married in the eyes of God."

He's giving me a way out. He's trying to soothe me by reassuring me that I've done nothing wrong. If I was just honest with him, he would know how terrible my thoughts truly are, and how little my willpower is.

I need God to forgive me. I need God to help me resist temptation. I need God to understand that I don't want my thoughts to go any further, but I'm only a man.

"No son of mine is going to be a fucking gay. Come here boy and I'll beat that shit right out of you."

My blood runs cold at the memory. My breaths come out in short uneven bursts. I mumble a prayer under my breath, praying away the pain, praying away the memories. The memories remind me just how terrible these feelings are—how *wrong* they are.

"Please, Father. This is all I can remember. I am sorry for these and all my sins," I recite, calling the words on how to end the confession and receive penance.

I can hear a sigh from the other side of the wall. "I suppose you should do two Our Fathers and three Hail Marys. Is this sufficient for you?"

No, it should be more. I should have to crawl on my knees to the altar and beg for forgiveness until my tongue falls off, but I gladly accept. "Yes, Father. Thank you."

"Now, I need to hear the prayer of sorrow."

"My God, I am sorry for my sins with all my heart. In choosing to do wrong and failing to do good, I have sinned against you…" I go through the rest of my prayer in my head, adding little bits here and there about how sorry I am and how much I need His strength. Once I'm done, Father Matteo gives me the prayer of Absolution, and my soul feels lighter.

I exit the booth after that and am immediately met by Father Matteo and his curious brown eyes. "Jarred, is everything okay?"

"Yes," I say, sweat beading my hairline at my obvious lie, and giving myself another reason to go through confession again. "I'm just…"

I can't finish my sentence, and Father Matteo seems to understand. He looks at me with compassion as he claps his hand on my shoulder and gives me a squeeze. "Look, son. If you ever want to talk to a friend and not your priest, I'm here for you. My door is always open to you."

I give him a lackluster smile. I don't plan on approaching him like a friend any time soon. That would be crossing yet another line that I'm not ready to face. Regardless, I appreciate the gesture. "Thank you, Father."

Although I feel a little bit of relief, the guilt still weighs heavily on my shoulders. It's only day one of camp, and I'm already lusting after someone I should never consider to be mine. I don't care how many confessions it takes.

I refuse to think of Noah Scott as anything other than my nineteen-year-old camp counselor.

CHAPTER 5
NOAH

As I sit in front of the bonfire, I can feel every twitch of my sore muscles.

While I'm happy I handed Bryce and Joshua their asses in flag foot-ball, I can admit that maybe I pushed myself a tiny bit too far. Well, fuck it, it was all worth it when I saw how happy Patrick looked when he scored his first touchdown.

It's night now, and all the counselors are sitting at our designated hangout area around a fire Kendall started. We're all just dicking around talking to each other, and it's kind of relaxing in a lowkey sort of way.

"Do you guys ever actually party?" I ask Patrick, reaching for a cigarette from my back pocket and lighting up.

He shakes his head from where he sits on the log beside me. "Um, not really? Mr. Walker doesn't let us have alcohol, even though most of us are old enough to drink. I think it would be a bad influence on the kids if they caught us."

I nod, relishing in the sweet burn of nicotine as I look around at the rest of the counselors. "Right because all of you are just so high and mighty. Perfect children who can do no wrong."

"I get that you don't want to be here, but would you mind not taking it out on me? I haven't exactly given you a reason to be a jerk to me."

I rear my head back at Patrick's words. So, the guy does have a backbone. I give him a slow smile, perching the cigarette in between my lips as I clap his back. "There he is. Sorry if I'm being an ass."

"It's okay, I get it," he says with a shrug. "My parents once sent me to football camp when I was ten. It was miserable. I think I cried myself to sleep every night."

I appreciate his honesty and try not to feel bad for him. I can see why Patrick would have been picked on his entire life. He's scrawny, wears these big glasses that take up too much of his face, and he's too shy for his own good. I think if he showed a little bit more of that sass he gave me, he'd have no problem standing up to Bryce and Joshua, or anybody else who fucks with him.

"Do you think I can...can try one of those?" he asks, pointing at my cigarette.

I raise a single brow. "You want to smoke? I have some weed in my pack back in the bunks."

"What? No. No drugs," he says, his face turning red. "I've just never had a cigarette before."

I shrug and hand him the one in between my lips. I only have a certain number of cigarettes, and I don't want to waste them if he completely hates it. "Help yourself."

He takes the cigarette gingerly between his fingers and flashes me a hesitant grin before taking a drag. I think it must go down the wrong hole or something because he immediately erupts in a fit of coughs so hard, I'm afraid he's going to burst a blood vessel.

"Take it easy," I say, rubbing his back as he continues to cough. "Maybe cigarettes just aren't your thing?"

"Aw, look at this. He's comforting his boyfriend. How cute."

I'm on my feet before I can think better of it. Bryce stands in front of Patrick and me, sneering at us with disgust. He must think he's absolutely hilarious, but I don't.

"Hop off, asshole," I snap, crowding his face as the rest of the group turns their gaze toward us. "What? Want me to suck your dick, Bryce?"

Bryce flushes and his fists clench by his side. "Fuck you. I don't want your lips anywhere near me."

"Then what's your fucking problem?" I ask, giving him a shove as he takes a step back. Bitch. "It's the first day of camp. Just leave us the fuck alone."

He shakes his head and laughs. "And where would be the fun in that? You two pussies are just too easy to rile up."

I'm not known for thinking before I act. I never have been. I think that's my excuse for why I lunge at Bryce, tackling him to the ground before I can think better of it.

He's all talk because when I raise my fist in the air and slam it down on the corner of his mouth, he doesn't do shit back. I can feel hands trying to pull me off him, but I've never been one to not finish what I start. Maybe a good ass-whooping is all it takes to get him to shut the fuck up. I could barely handle his big mouth for one day, so I don't think I could take it for another three months.

Fists land on my temple, something hard hitting my side. I go down flat on my back, and I throw my hands up in front of my face just in time for Joshua to land a solid punch to my outstretched hands. I scramble onto my feet, fist poised in the air, ready to fucking retaliate, but a voice breaks through my violent haze.

"The three of you! Stop!"

I stumble as I turn and face Jarred who's absolutely red with anger. His eyes dart between me, Joshua, and Bryce as he starts putting the pieces together. He marches up to the three of us, his veins jutting out of his forehead as he points at Bryce and Joshua. "You two. My office! Five a.m. tomorrow! The rest of you, go to bed!" I start to turn and walk away with the rest of the crowd until a hand on the crook of my elbow stops me. "Not *you*. You're coming with me."

I groan as Jarred drags me away from the bonfire. He takes long strides that I struggle to catch up with as we head to the center of the camp. It isn't until we pass the mess hall that I realize he's taking me to the infirmary.

"This isn't necessary," I argue, trying to pull my arm away from him, but he has me in a grasp of steel.

"Don't speak," he growls, all but pushing me into the infirmary and slamming the door shut behind him. "I don't want to hear you speak for at least five minutes. Now sit down and let me look at you."

I hesitantly take a seat on one of the beds they have set up here, twiddling with my thumbs, but shooting him an angry glare as I do. I'm only following his directions because it's better than bitch fighting with him right now.

"I didn't think I needed to say it this morning, but fighting is against the rules," he states, violently rummaging through the drawers until he finds what he's looking for and pulls out some packets and gauze. "What were you thinking?"

"You want me to speak—"

"Be quiet!" He tears open one of the packets and stands between my spread legs, gripping my chin and angling my head back and forth. "A split eyebrow and a bloody lip. Do you think this is how I want my camp to be represented?"

"Well, not really—"

"Five minutes is not up! I'm going to get you patched up and then, and only then, can you speak!"

I nod and keep my mouth shut. I didn't think Jarred had this in him. He's so pissed off right now, his brown eyes like steel as he wipes away some blood from my eyebrow—careful to avoid my piercing— and puts some type of ointment around it. Next, he moves on to my mouth, and I must be imagining the way he discreetly plays with the ring on my bottom lip. He cleans me up, his hands far gentler than his tone, and I can appreciate it.

"What got into you?" he asks, taking a step back and discarding his supplies in the trashcan. "What were you thinking?"

I raise my injured brow and scoff. "Can I speak now?"

"Not with that attitude."

"Fine," I groan, my fists clenched around the paper blanket beneath me. "Bryce was being a dick and bullying Patrick. All I did was stand up for him which is more than I can say for you."

"What?" he questions, narrowing his eyes at me. "What did I do?"

"Nothing. You did nothing. Those guys have been picking on him for *years*, and you just casually didn't notice?" I seethe, ignoring how close he's getting to me.

His jaw drops lightly, and all traces of anger are gone with confusion taking its place. "He's been getting bullied? Here?"

"Yeah," I say, tipping my head to the side as I read his expression. "You really didn't know?"

"How could I have? Bryce and Joshua have been nothing but outstanding counselors."

I snort. "That just shows how much you know about the people that work for you, old man."

"Just because you're angry with me, doesn't mean you get to be disrespectful," he snaps, leaning forward and planting both hands on either side of my hips. His hot breath fans my lips as he leans forward, eyes narrowed with danger and something else I can't quite place. "Apologize."

I suck in a little breath but hold my ground. Am I being a brat? Yes. Do I care? "No."

"Why are you so angry?" he questions as he lifts his hand to trace the cut on my eyebrow. "Look where your anger got you, son."

"I'm not your son," I snap, slapping his hand away. "I have no idea why the fuck you picked me, but I don't want to be here. *That's* why I'm angry. I don't want to be here, but if I have to be here, I'm not just going to stand by and let people get picked on by those pricks."

"Why are you here then?" he asks, cocking his head to the side as he leans in closer. "Why don't you just go home if you already hate it so much?"

"Because I need this," I admit through gritted teeth. "If I want to stay at UNC, I need to spend the entire fucking summer here."

His fingers once again find my lips. "Watch your mouth."

"Or what?"

He drops his head and his hand as he takes in a deep shuddering breath, his shoulders rising and falling with the tension he carries. He's white-knuckling the paper sheet underneath us and I can feel the way his arms tremble. He takes a hard step back and shakes his head. "Fine. You don't want to be here, and I understand. But if you want to stay, you have to cut the attitude. Maybe if you actually tried to enjoy yourself, you'd realize this place isn't that bad."

I scoff and gesture down at my ripped jeans and band t-shirt. "Do I look like I fit in here?"

"All I'm asking is for you to try," he whispers, his eyes wandering down my figure and averting his gaze at the last second. "Just try or go home."

I'd love to go home. I'd love to forget this shitty day and put this whole weird experience behind me, but I can't. If I want to keep going to UNC, I have to do this. UNC is my safe haven, my happy place. I love my classes, I love my dorm, and I love my friends. It's the one place in my entire life I've felt free to be myself. It's the one place I can escape my shit-bag parents and just be me.

And I'll do anything it takes to keep that, even if it means pretending to pray to Jesus and ignoring my unusual attraction to my camp director.

"Okay," I finally say.

His eyes widen. "Okay?"

"Yeah, okay. I'll…" I clench my jaw but nod. "I'll try."

The smile Jarred gives me rocks through me. It's so full of kindness and optimism, the exact opposite of how I feel, and it makes my chest all tingly. "Wonderful. Tomorrow is kind of a day for the counselors to hang out and get to know each other, but we need to get your lifeguard training sorted. How about you meet me at the lake around seven?"

I bite the corner of my lip, tongue playing with my lip ring as I nod. "Sure thing, boss."

His eyes trace the way my tongue flickers against the cool silver hoop and gulps. "Um, okay. Good. I'll see you tomorrow, Noah."

And he hightails it out of the room without another word before I can say anything else.

And if I'm not mistaken, that might be lust I saw in his eyes.

CHAPTER 6
NOAH

I drag my ass out of bed at seven in the morning, annoyed that Patrick gets to sleep in, but satisfied when I see that Bryce and Joshua are missing. I peel off my clothes and dress in the only pair of swim trunks I brought. I grab a cigarette from the pack in the back of the pants I wore last night and light up as I exit the cabin. It only takes me a few minutes to get to the lake, and Jarred is already at the dock waiting for me.

I give him an appreciative sweep of my eyes before he can notice me checking him out.

Damn, he's hot as fuck.

There's some blonde hair on his chest that leads down to a happy trail that disappears into his blue trunks, blue trunks that fit him like a second skin and do delicious things to his ass. The veins in his arms bulge as he pulls a board out of the water, and I lick my lips when he stretches out his arms and shows off that tight fucking body.

Yeah, his wife is crazy for thinking he's anything other than smoking hot.

"Jarred," I say, approaching him as I take a drag of my cigarette. "Looking good this morning."

He blushes and it creeps down from his cheek to his neck. His eyes widen slightly as he takes in my chest—probably not used to seeing guys with their nipples pierced—and his eyes immediately look toward the sky. He does that a lot around me, avert his gaze, and I want to find out why.

But I guess that can wait until I've learned how to save a life.

"Um, yeah, thanks," he mumbles, running a large hand through his thick hair. He looks at the cigarette in my hand and frowns. "You know you're not supposed to be smoking, right?"

"Yup," I nod, taking a deliberate drag from it. "And?"

He still looks a bit flustered, his eyes continuously tracking down to my pierced nipples. He shakes his head and coughs as he leans down and picks up a whistle from the ground before handing it to me. "So, this will be quick. I just need to make sure that you have your first aid training done and that you're a good enough swimmer to be on lake duty."

I nod and put out my cigarette under my flip-flop, taking the whistle from him. "Sounds cool. Where do we start?"

And from there starts the long odious process of first aid training.

First, we start with the basics of how to identify a concussion, heat stroke, and sudden cardiac arrest. He shows me the portable defibrillator that stays at the lifeguard hut and teaches me how to use it. After that, he shows me how to give chest compressions on a plastic dummy. Then we talk about the different rescue equipment and how to properly determine the best way to enter the water. Finally, we move on to the rescue skills.

"So, it's pretty simple," he says, taking a step back so he's standing at the edge of the dock. "We have to go through escapes and rescue techniques. For this example, I'll get into the water and act as a distressed swimmer. Your job is to make sure that you and I make it back to the shore in one piece. I'm going to start off by being a passive drowning victim."

I nod and watch as he smiles before jumping into the lake. He swims out far enough that it'll take me a decent swim to get to him before turning over on his front and pretending like he's unconscious.

I recall the entry method he taught me and enter the water in a dive, making sure to limit the energy that I put into my strokes and that my rescue tube rests securely on my chest. Once I reach him, I come at him from behind and roll him face up, putting his head in my hands and the rescue tube under his arms as I swim back to the shore.

I try not to get distracted by how big and strong he feels in my arms. I focus on just getting him to safety and ignoring how my dick is screaming at me to rub into the crease of his ass. Thankfully, it's easy enough to drag him onto the sand and lay him on his back.

Once we're back on dry ground, he sits up and gives me a cheesy thumbs-up. "That was great, Noah. This next one is going to be a bit tough. I'm going to be thrashing around and you have to make sure you think of yourself as well as you try to attempt a rescue."

I nod and watch him get back into the water, swimming to the same exact spot he was in earlier. This time, however, he's acting like a panicked victim. He's kicking and waving his hands in the air, and I already know this isn't going to be easy. I head back into the water and go for the front approach this time, testing it out to see if it's better suited for this kind of rescue.

When I get to him, he's still a panicked mess, and he surprises me by wrapping his thick legs around my waist and trying to drag me down into the water.

"Fuck, Jarred," I growl, trying to dislodge him from me as he continues to grab on. "Don't make this too fucking difficult."

He just laughs at that and dunks me under the water. "Come on, Noah. You have to save me."

"Debatable," I snort as I try to find the best way to carry him while he's trying to drown me. This might make him uncomfortable, but I settle for resting my hands on his bubble ass and pulling him closer to me. "Don't let go."

I can feel the deep breath he sucks in, and I try to hold back my own laugh. If he wanted to be difficult, this is what's going to happen. I'm going to get a nice juicy handful of this amazing ass. I'm not a creep though, so I just rest my hands there, even though they're dying to knead into those firm cheeks. He tries to release himself from my hold, but that's not how a rescue works. If I let him go, I fail the lifeguard training, and I'm committed now.

"Just relax," I whisper into his ear, pulling him tighter against me. "We're almost to the shore."

I'll admit that it's fucking hard to swim with him this way, but I feel a sharp thrill of victory when we make it to the bank of the lake in one piece. He's heavy as fuck, but I manage to carry him and lay him down on the sand.

I hover over him for a second and, fuck, he's so fucking hot. His cheeks are burning red, and he has this hesitant look in his eyes as I check his pulse with my fingers. But there's something underneath that. There's a hot tension there I can't and won't ignore.

He swallows hard. "That was a good job. We should—"

"But what if you were passed out?" I question, already moving my hands to cup his cheeks because I just can't fucking help myself. "We didn't go over mouth-to-mouth."

"Oh, well, we—" He lets out a shuddering breath, hands itching at his side and digging into the sand. "You'd...um...tip my chin back."

"Like this?" I ask, tipping his chin back just a little, giving his lips the perfect angle to reach mine. I lean forward just a bit, brushing my nose against his. "What would I do next?"

"We don't..." He shakes his head as his nose grazes mine. "The dummy is—"

"You're right here," I whisper sultrily, thumbing his mouth until it opens for me. "Might as well get some practical experience. What do I do next, Jarred?"

"You..." He gulps, his breaths shaky against my mouth. He swipes his tongue over his bottom lip, grazing mine and making me groan. "You put your mouth on me."

When he doesn't pull away or shove me off him, I shoot my shot. My lips come down over his as I breathe into his mouth. The contact is magnetic and fiery, forcing me to press my full weight on him as I pretend to breathe life back into him. I'm rewarded with a little whimper as I take my chance and trail my tongue along his bottom lip, relishing in the taste of lake water and *him*. I feel a dangerous jolt of heat when I feel him chub up against my crotch, and I barely resist the urge to grind my hips down on his.

He wants this. I wasn't necessarily messing with him, but I didn't think he'd react like *this*. He's growing hard for me, needy for me, and it makes me turn the simple exercise into a full-blooded kiss.

I growl into his mouth, all pretenses gone, and hold his face in my hands. I let my full body weight drop, I blanket him, and I even fucking dry hump him because holy shit this is the hottest kiss of my entire life. He's so strong underneath me, so sturdy, so extremely unwavering.

He hesitates into the kiss until he gently nips at my lips and his hands come up to wrap around my back. As we kiss, they migrate all over my body, greedy hands that just can't get enough. When he brings them to my nipples and plays with my sensitive piercings, I pull back with a rough curse.

"You're so fucking hot," I say, dragging my teeth down the side of his neck. "God, Jarred. *Fuck yes.*"

I don't know what snaps him out of it, but in a matter of seconds, I'm roughly shoved off him and fall ass first into the sand. He bolts up, hands coming up to touch his lips as he shakes his head. I can see the panic filling his terrified dark eyes.

"Hey," I say gently as I approach him. "It's okay. It was—"

"No!" he shouts, frantically looking around as he takes wide steps back from me. "No! I can't! I'm not..."

"No, you're totally not," I say, trying to appease him. "But we should talk about it."

"There's nothing to talk about!" he snaps, running his hand furiously through his hair. "I've—I've got to go."

I take a step forward and reach out to him. "Jarred, wait—"

"No!"

His agonized shout is all I hear as he literally runs away from me. I'm left a panting mess, entirely turned on, and feeling like a jerk. I sit my ass down and drop my head into my hands.

I didn't pressure him, did I? Did I give him a chance to say no? A chance to shove me away? I feel a mixture of guilt and humiliation at my actions. I'd never want him to feel like I pressured him into anything, but his body didn't lie. He was hard, he was into it—

And it felt like he wanted me just as much as I wanted him.

CHAPTER 7
JARRED

"No, no, no, no..." I mumble to myself as I crash through the front door of my cabin.

I can't believe that happened. I can't believe Noah actually kissed me. There are a million and one reasons why that shouldn't have happened—he's my counselor and he's nineteen—but the most important one is that he's a *man*.

The worst part is that I let it happen. I wanted it. I slipped. Lord, forgive me. I slipped. I slipped and I let him kiss me. I let him run his tongue across my lips. I let him taste the inside of my mouth. I let him hold me in his arms. And I hate the fact that it felt...

No, it couldn't have felt right. It didn't. I've spent forty-five years of my life only engaging in sexual activity with women, and I'd rather lose my camp than let that happen again.

It was just a slip because, *Lord,* I'm only human. I couldn't resist the temptation when it was dangling right in front of me.

And what a temptation it was.

When he had me pressed against the bank, his lean young body blanketing mine, all sense of reason disappeared. The sun was bouncing off all his piercings and making them glitter. He was wet and half naked and dripping for me. His nipples—his freaking *nipples*—

were pierced and it's one of the hottest things I've ever seen. Hotter than any lingerie Jenny ever wore and any porn I'd ever watched.

My cock likes the memory of it way too much. I try to hold myself back, but I can't. I'm only human, and I have urges that I can't deny. Like the urge to shove down my trunks and wrap my hand around my cock.

I close my eyes as I brace myself against the front door. The reality is that the kiss was tame in comparison to the things I've stopped myself from picturing, but I can't stop the wayward thoughts now.

I want to feel that lip ring trail against my stiff length. I want those sweet lips that tasted of stale cigarettes wrapped around me, sucking me to the back of his throat, puffy and wet and coated with my cum. I want to fall on my knees for him and lick every inch of his pale body. I want his fingers stuffed in me, his cock splitting me in half, I want it all.

It's pure and carnal lust. It was an immediate attraction that drew me to him, but I also want more. I want to know what makes him so bitter, so angry. I want to know the things I could do to make him smile. I want to be the reason he smiles.

My breaths are coming out uneven and ragged like I've just run a mile as I come all over my hand. My legs feel like jelly as I let myself collapse against the door. Before I can stop it, I'm sobbing into my hands. I can't want this. The memories of the last time I let myself stray come back to assault me.

"Is that what you want, son? Tell me and I'll show you just how sick you are!

No, I can't. I can't do this. I can't.

I get up and jump into the shower, roughly scrubbing at my hands and my dick despite the pain. I need to feel the pain. I need to be punished.

I sob into my hands, letting the shower water drip down my mouth, choking me. At some point, my legs can no longer hold me, and I collapse into myself onto the shower floor.

I got myself off on Noah, and it was a mistake that God will judge me for.

CHAPTER 8
NOAH

It's a whirlwind of chaos around me as the campers exit their ugly yellow buses and make their way down the winding path toward the camp entrance. There must be at least a hundred of them—all eager and excited—and I don't think I stopped to realize how popular this place is.

"Isn't this awesome?" Kendall asks, bouncing on her feet as she claps her hands. "Look at them all! This is going to be the best summer ever!"

I raise my pierced brow as I look at her bubblegum pink 'Jesus Loves You' T-shirt with the camp logo on the back and then cringe when I look down at my matching bright yellow one. "The greatest."

She narrows her eyes at me as she slaps my arm with her clipboard. "Enough with the attitude, Noah. The campers will notice."

"I think that's his point," Patrick snorts, pushing his thick glasses up his nose. He fidgets with his own clipboard and gulps when the noise of the campers nears us. "I always hate the first day."

"Really? I love it!"

"As if that weren't obvious," I snark, but only half-heartedly. In the last week, I've grown to like Kendall and Patrick. They're weird and quirky in their own endearing way. Kendall, for all her bubbly enthusiasm, is wicked smart. Patrick, while quiet, has a funny sense of humor.

I never thought I'd actually make friends here, but it does take away from how awful this experience will be.

"Here they come!"

All the counselors take a step back and form a straight shoulder-to-shoulder line as the campers crowd around us. Jarred's there, front and center, with a huge smile plastered on his face. He looks so proud, so happy, and it does weird things to my stomach.

"These are your counselors!" Jarred shouts loud enough for everyone to hear. "We'll be calling you up and they'll show you where your bunk is!"

He goes through the list of counselors and, slowly but surely, the hoard of children thins out as they all follow their people to their bunks. When I'm the last one standing, Jarred turns to me briefly before speaking. "Noah. The rest of these campers are yours."

I hate the fact that his voice is strained and that he can barely look at me as he speaks.

I take a tentative step forward, and I can't miss the way he side-steps me when I get too close to him. I click my tongue as I wave my hand at the campers.

Things have been tense between us. In the last week, Jarred's been so flighty around me. Every time I get anywhere near him, he acts like he has something else to do and flees. I can't get him to make eye contact with me for more than a few seconds. Everything he has to say to me has been going through Kendall, and I think she's too adorably clueless to question why.

"Thanks, boss," I mumble, messing with my lip ring as I gesture at the campers to follow me. "Let's go."

The campers and I make our way through the center of the camp to the right side of the property where their bunks are located. I took a look at them yesterday and, if it's even possible, they're smaller than ours. I ignore all their questions as I give them the tour, mumbling and murmuring my way through it as my interaction with Jarred lingers in the back of my mind.

It was just one kiss. One *hot, steamy* kiss but a kiss, nonetheless. I realized two seconds after I had kissed him that it had been a mistake. I had no right to approach him like that or even suggest giving him mouth-to-mouth. I had been so stupid and so reckless. That interaction revolved around what I wanted, and I hadn't even considered that he wouldn't want the same thing.

I itch for a cigarette as I finish up the tour and jut my thumb at the bunks behind me. "Okay, here it is. Boys in Bunk Four and girls in Bunk Five. Lunch is in an hour. Lights out at nine. Don't annoy me and I won't bug you."

I go to leave the slightly confused campers, but one of them decides to jump in front of me at the last second. He's tiny, maybe around thirteen years old, and he reminds me of Patrick with his oversized glasses and his even more oversized shirt. "Um, Noah?"

I raise my pierced brow at him and decide, fuck it, I'll have a cigarette. "Yes...?"

"Ian," he says. His eyes widen when he sees me light my cigarette, but they snap back to me a second later. "My name is Ian."

"Okay, what's up, Ian?"

He shifts from one foot to another and chews on his bottom lip. "Can I call my parents?"

I resist the urge to roll my eyes. I don't want to deal with a kid who's getting cold feet at the very last second. "We don't have landlines available to the campers, just mail," I drone, playing back Kendall's earlier instructions on what to say in this situation. "You'll have to write them a letter."

He stutters a response, pushing his crooked glasses up the bridge of his nose. "But—"

"Anything else?" I snap, taking a deep drag of both my cigarette and relief as he shakes his head. "Awesome."

I leave the campers behind in a huff as I walk back in the direction of my bunk. I have an hour of free time before I'm supposed to be supervising lunch, and I need a fucking joint. I already have my mind set on jogging down to the dock for a quick toke until I spot something in the corner of my eye.

Jarred.

He's on his own, diligently checking off the list on his clipboard as he heads into one of the storage huts just on the edge of the woods. His back is hunched over tight and he's not even looking where he's going as he enters the hut.

This is my shot. I just need to clear the air with him. If I have to spend three months in this fucking hell hole, I'm not doing it with this weird energy between us. We're both adults—albeit he's more of an adult than I am—and we can move past this. I give a quick check over my shoulder as I run up to the hut, checking to see if anybody has noticed me, and slip in undetected.

"Hey."

Jarred has his back to me and his head whips around at the sound of my voice. He drops his clipboard as his cheeks flame pink and his mouth drops open. He gathers his bearings quickly and bends down to retrieve his clipboard, all the while hissing at me. "What are you doing here? Someone will see you."

"Talking to my boss?" I question sarcastically, reaching down when I see he hasn't picked up his pen. "No one's going to say shit."

I hand him his pen, but he doesn't thank me. Instead, he takes one large step back and his panicked eyes look over my shoulder. "You should go."

"We need to talk about what happened."

"Nothing happened."

"You know that's not true." I sigh. "That kiss—"

He shakes his head and turns his back on me again, checking some supplies on the shelf in front of us. "I don't know what you're talking about."

"You can't just ignore it and pretend like it didn't happen. Don't be —" I cut myself off and take off my beanie, running my hands through my hair in frustration. I take a deep breath and reach out to touch his shoulder. "Look, I'm sorry if I made you uncomfortable. If you want me to back off, I'll back off."

Under my touch, I can feel the muscles in his taut back quiver. The shaky sound of his clipboard hitting the metal rack rings loud in the small space as his hands tremble. "It's…"

"What?" I whisper and, emboldened by his body's response to me, take a step forward.

He turns around slowly and watches my hands as they drop to my side. He doesn't look up at me as he licks his lip, his chest heaving up and down with strain. "It's not about...wanting it."

So, he did want me. I was right. I didn't just attack him without him wanting it too. Although this should make me happy and relieved, it does nothing to quell the nagging guilt in my mind. He might have wanted it, but he regrets it. That might be just as bad as not wanting it at all.

I can't even imagine what's going on in his brain. I can't picture what he must be feeling. He's obviously catholic to the max—the camp he set up demonstrates that—and he must be confused about what happened between us. I don't want to add to that confusion despite how badly I want him.

"It was just a kiss, Jarred. A hot, sexy ass, mouthwatering kiss, but a kiss," I say, trying to reassure him. "We can pretend like it never happened after today."

He looks up at me and gulps audibly, nodding. "I think that would be for the best. It was a mistake, and it shouldn't have happened. It was...it was *wrong*."

It shouldn't have happened because he's my boss. It shouldn't have happened because he has to be two decades older than I am. It shouldn't have happened because he's not entirely sure who he is.

Not because it was wrong like he said. Not because it was disgusting like he's suggesting. Not because it's a fucking sin like the fucking church has taught him.

"I agree," I start, feeling my brows set into a pinch. "Maybe not for the same reasons you do."

He narrows his eyes at me as his jaw forms a tight angry line. "I'm not gay."

"I never said you were," I say, raising my hands in the air to appease him. "I'm bi, so I get it—"

"No. None of that," he snaps, his lips curled in disgust as he pinches the bridge of his nose. "I'm straight. One hundred percent straight."

"I don't want to be a dick, Jarred, but it sure didn't feel like that," I snort, barely able to keep the sarcasm out of my voice.

"What did it..." His face cools and his shoulders drop. I don't know if he realizes it, but he's moved closer to me. He licks his plump lips slowly, and I wonder if he knows just how fucking tempting that is. "What did it feel like?"

I raise both brows at that. "You really want to know?"

It takes him a second, but he slowly nods, and I can't and won't ignore the way his eyes stay fixated on my lip ring. "Yes."

I was content to just lay everything out on the table and pretend the kiss never happened. I was okay with not adding to his confusion and walking away. I was even fine with him resigning himself to live in denial, but now I'm not.

He's asking me to tell him what that kiss did to me, what it felt like to be pressed up against him, and maybe he's asking me this because he can't bear to say it himself.

"It felt like...you wanted it to happen," I whisper, drawing my eyes up and down his figure as I take up his space. "I don't know if you realized it at the time, but those cute little whimpers you let out in my mouth turned me the fuck on. It's like you were begging me to kiss you, begging me to touch you, maybe even begging me to fuck you."

He stutters out a breath and I can see a faint sheen of sweat lining his forehead. "No, I could never..."

"My wet chest pressed against yours and all that sticky skin felt amazing," I breathe, closing my eyes in remembrance of his damp skin dragging against mine. I crowd him just a little bit more until his back hits the metal racks behind him. "I could almost feel the ridges of your cock as I ground myself against you. If I had kept dry fucking you, would you have come in your pants?"

"I—I've never..."

"Never what, Jarred? Come in your pants?" I ask, gently lifting one finger to trace it down his chest, fingering one of his pant loops as I pull him flush against me. "You've never gotten yourself wet and messy, so fucking turned on you couldn't wait to whip that dick out and beat it?"

He groans and drops his head back and the metal rattles violently. He might not notice that his hips are rolling in the air, seeking out my body, seeking out relief. "Noah..."

"What do you want? You want me to kiss you?" I tease, leaning forward to rest my lips against his ear. "You want me to touch you?" I give his earlobe a gentle tug with my teeth. "Just give me the word, Jarred, and I'll suck you so good."

His hands latch onto my shoulders, but he doesn't push me off. "I don't want it."

"Don't? This cock tells me a different story," I say, finally giving into my body's needs and rubbing my thumb up and down his crotch, his hard cock tenting the material.

"Can't!" he shouts, his voice breaking at the word. He sucks in a sharp breath and scrambles away from me, holding his clipboard over his clothed dick as he reaches for the doorknob. "I *can't* want it!"

Before I get a chance to say anything, he's out of the hut. He's leaving a trail of sex and lust in his wake, and I palm my cock over my pants at the serious blue balls I've given myself. Sure, he's in denial, but there's no way in hell he's straight.

And just maybe he wants me to help him see that.

CHAPTER 9
NOAH

I'm exhausted. Who knew that Catholics had such high stamina?

My smoker's lungs burn as I make my way back to my bunk. We took the new campers on a hike around the lake, and nobody bothered to tell me that said hike would take *four hours*. Four fucking hours in the middle of nowhere, surrounded by pre-teens, preyed on by bugs and getting dirt where dirt should never go.

"Noah!"

I turn around to the counselor who called my name. Grace, I think? She runs up to me, hair in a perfect ponytail, looking like we didn't just walk twelve miles. "'Sup."

She bounces on her heels in front of me as she flutters her eyelashes. "Have any plans for later tonight?"

She's cute. Dark hair, deep brown eyes, a nice soft waist that leads to a nice-looking ass. I'd totally be all over her if it weren't for the fact that I feel like dying on the spot.

And…

I shake my head as I lift my shirt to wipe some sweat off my upper lip. "Sleeping off this day sounds nice."

"You should come to the party we're having," she says, laughing as if I've said something hilarious.

"Party?"

"Yeah. Nicky snuck some booze in from town." When she takes in my slightly startled expression, she snorts. "What? Did you think we were all goody-two-shoes like Kendall?"

I ignore the subtle jab at Kendall and consider it. Despite feeling like my legs are going to fall off, kicking back and letting loose sounds nice. If they have booze, and I have weed, that's a nice combo to end the day. "I guess. Where's it at?"

"On the other side of the lake. Just take the path that winds around the lake and veer left when you see the rock shaped like a dick." She stops and grabs onto my wrist. "Oh, and don't tell Kendall about this."

I tip my head to the side. "Why?"

She rolls her eyes as if it's obvious before scoffing. "Because she's the bunk leader, and she'll rat us out to her perfect Mr. Walker. You have to wait until she does her bunk checks and then you can go."

Yeah, Kendall would totally try and stop me. I like the girl, but she can be a bit heavy-handed with her responsibilities. "Alright. I'm in."

"Awesome! I'll see you then," Grace says, and I don't miss the way she winks at me before skipping away toward her giggling friends.

I chuckle lightly at myself as I trudge up the stairs to my bunk, kicking the door open weakly with my foot. I resist the urge to just collapse on my bed when Patrick comes in. And he, just like everyone else apparently, looks fine.

"Hey, man. What's up?" I ask him as I peel off my shirt and toss it in the dirty hamper we keep by our bunk beds.

He blushes as he eyes me, his eyes flickering up and down my figure before they land on the ceiling. He shrugs and climbs up the ladder to his bed. "Nothing. I'm thinking I'm going to just read and turn in early tonight."

"Want a change of scenery?" I suggest. "There's a party on the other side of the lake."

"Oh…" he says, scrunching up his nose as he reaches for his book. "*Those.*"

I stop halfway through pulling down my pants. "You mean you know about them?"

"Everyone does, well, not Kendall," he corrects himself. "Grace always organizes a couple every summer."

"Have you ever been?"

"I've actually never been invited," he murmurs, chewing on his bottom lip as he fingers a random page in his book. It doesn't surprise me that no one's ever invited him. Patrick's wound up so tight that he always looks like he's two seconds away from snapping.

"Fuck that. I'm inviting you," I say, and then I add. "If you want to go, that is."

There's a tentative smile on his lips as he considers it. After a moment, he puts down his book and nods. "Um, yeah. It sounds like fun?"

I chuckle at his *incredible* enthusiasm and grab a towel, my shower shoes, and my shower caddy. "Okay. I'm gonna hit the showers and then we can wait for Kendall to check in before we go."

He nods. "Okay."

I up nod at him before leaving the bunk. The showers are kept about a three-minute walk away from where we sleep. It's the most rustic-looking shower I've ever been in. It's just a few wooden stalls with curtains for privacy. I hook my towel on the rack beside the curtain and step in. The water is ice cold when I turn it on, and it takes longer than I like for it to turn into some sort of lukewarm spray. I set my shower caddy on the floor and root through my products, shampooing and conditioning my hair quickly because the warm water is sure to not last.

It's when I get to the body wash that the urge to wrap my hand around my dick resurfaces. I've been sporting a semi for most of the day, still caught up in my earlier exchange with Jarred. Although he was skittish and although he was unsure, he was so fucking turned on.

He looked so adorable—a big strong man weak in the knees for me —and it got to me in a way I hadn't expected. I didn't kiss him, didn't even touch him really, but the slightest contact we had left my skin burning pleasantly. The air was so erotically charged, so sticky with hot tension, and my cock remembers it all too well.

I give myself a few tugs and decide to let off some steam. This place is the only area in the camp where we get even a semblance of privacy, flimsy curtain aside.

As I reach down and roll my balls in my hand, a myriad of dirty images flood my brain. My imagination is wild with the ideas I have for Jarred. I wonder if he'll like being on his knees for me, or if the pink on his cheeks extends to other parts of his body, and if he'll be eager for my cock.

I imagine that he'll beautifully present himself to me. He'll be a greedy little cock slut for sure, bending over and spreading his cheeks. Maybe I can even get him to play with himself in front of me, to shove some of those thick fingers into his hole, and get himself ready for me.

I bite my bottom lip painfully, muffling my groans as my hand speeds up. Will he whimper? Will he cry out for me? Will he beg me to get him off?

Will he take what I give him with a please and thank you?

That thought sets me off, and I come against the shower wall. As I breathe deeply, the water washes away any evidence of my solo session. That's what it is and will probably only be—a solo session.

Despite wanting it, I don't think Jarred will ever cave to what he really wants. Despite the arousal in his deep brown eyes, he had been scared. I've been with guys in the closet, and I don't think I want to do that again.

After years of being disregarded and mistreated by my asshole parents, I've decided that I'm no one's dirty secret.

I quickly finish washing just as the water turns freezing. I step out and wrap my towel around my waist, gathering my supplies and heading back to the bunks. Sure, I get some weird looks from the counselors as I walk half-naked through the woods, but I don't give a fuck. I've never been shy or ashamed.

Patrick and I end up waiting over two hours before Kendall finally comes to check in with us. We give her a half-assed lie about going to bed early, and she accepts it eagerly as she goes to find Bryce and Joshua. Fuckers didn't even bother to make an excuse about where they are, and I can only assume they're already at the party.

We head over there, using flashlights to guide our way in the dark, and I snicker when I see that the rock is indeed shaped like a dick.

Once we round the corner, a bonfire appears and almost every counselor is gathered around it. Red solo cups litter the floor and the smell of booze and sweat permeates the air.

Just my kind of scene.

"I'll get us some drinks," I tell Patrick over the music, giving him a little shoulder check as I head to the makeshift bar. I pour myself a generous amount of some sort of pineapple vodka and soda while skimping on Patrick's a bit. I can only guess that he's not a drinker, and I don't want him trashed by the end of this.

"Is that for your boyfriend?"

I roll my eyes as I turn to Bryce and sigh. "Look, I don't know why you're so obsessed with me, but it's best to just leave me alone unless you want your ass kicked again."

He snorts and snatches a bottle of rum off the table. "I don't have to resort to that to get what I want. Just fucking watch your back, you freak."

I honestly have no idea what Bryce's problem is with me. I turn and leave him with those parting words. If he thinks he can get to me, he's wrong. He can sling however many insults he wants as long as he doesn't fuck with my friends.

I see Patrick in the corner of the party, awkwardly twiddling with his fingers as he waits for me to come back. He looks so lost and out of place, so tentative as he makes some sort of weird attempt at dancing, but it's endearing all on its own.

I smile because, yeah, friends sound okay.

"Here," I say, handing him his cup when I reach him. "I didn't put too much in it, so you should get a nice buzz."

He smiles as he accepts the cup and takes a little sip. "Thanks, Noah."

We stand there for a bit and just watch the party unfold around us. Damn, how did I forget that Catholic teenagers can party? Everyone's drinking, beer pong is set up by the bonfire—which is a stupid choice —and couples are grinding together to the beat of the song playing in the background.

If this is what camp is like, I might not hate it as much as I thought I would.

When I reach into my jacket and pull out the rolled joint I brought, Patrick gasps. "Is that marijuana?"

"Yeah, it's just a little weed," I tell him as I pull out my lighter from the pocket of my beanie. He looks at the joint intensely and I laugh. "You want some?"

"Will it...?"

"What?" I ask, lighting up and taking a deep drag, holding it in my lungs for a second before blowing it out.

"What does it feel like?"

"Really fucking good, man," I laugh, already feeling the premium bud kick in. "No pressure, but you can have some if you want."

When he reaches for the joint, I pause. I take a look around and see that no one's noticed I've sparked up yet, and I want to keep it that way. It's not that I'm against sharing, but I only brought so much weed with me to last me through the end of camp. I don't mind sharing with Patrick, but everybody else can fuck off. "Here, come with me."

Patrick willingly follows me into the woods, not too far from the others, but far enough where they won't notice us. I take a seat on a large boulder and hand him the joint. He stares at it for a second before taking a drag. Then another. Then another in such a quick succession that he coughs like he's hacking a lung out.

"Woah, man. It's puff puff pass," I tease, taking the joint away from his trembling fingers as his face turns red. "Take it easy."

"S—Sorry," he coughs, giggling at himself. "Got ahead of myself."

We pass the joint around like that until it's almost gone. He looks like he's high as fuck, and I realize maybe I should have limited him to just a few puffs. "How you feeling?"

His eyes are glossy and red as he gives me a slurred smile. "Great."

"You're soaring, man," I chuckle, feeling myself getting closer and closer to being slightly trashed as I down my drink.

"I've never done anything fun before," he admits, jumping on the boulder beside me as he swings his legs, more at ease than I've ever seen him before.

I wrinkle my brows. "How old are you?"

"Twenty-one," he says with a little laugh. "I've never gotten drunk, never smoked, never really done anything fun." He sighs and drops his face into his hands. "I'm so lame."

I give his shoulder a nudge. "Don't say that."

"What would you call it? I mean, look at you," he says, waving wildly up and down my figure.

"What about me?"

"You're so...I don't know? Cool?"

"I'm not cool, man," I scoff. "Trust me, you don't want my life."

I may seem down to earth up front, but Patrick has no idea how messed up my life actually is. Sure, I have it pretty sweet at UNC, but my parents are a nightmare.

I understand that I'm lucky enough to have parents who pay for my college, but that's all they do. Growing up, they didn't give one single shit about me if it didn't involve going to church or getting perfect grades. The standards they set for me were too high to ever reach and, instead of loving me anyway, I didn't exist if I didn't act like they wanted me to.

I know people have it rough. I know my sob story is nothing to cry about. I know life is hard for everyone, but I can't imagine Patrick having anything but loving parents—albeit maybe parents who sheltered him too much.

"Hey, Noah?"

I turn to Patrick who suddenly looks so serious. He's worrying his bottom lip as he gently places the joint I just gave him on the boulder. "Yeah? What are you—"

And he surprises the shit out of me by launching himself at me and attacking my lips with his.

I'm in shock for a few seconds, feeling his chapped lips brush against mine and his sweaty palms cradle my cheeks, and I don't have the chance to do anything before he rips himself away with a pained shout.

"Oh! Oh no!" he yells, standing up and running his fingers through his hair. "Oh, I'm so sorry! I shouldn't have done that."

Now that I've sobered up a bit and gotten over my surprise, I shake my head. He looks absolutely mortified and he has no reason to be. I don't really like him like that, and I never imagined he was into dudes, but I don't want him to feel bad. "What? No, it's fine."

"It's not fine."

And my blood runs cold as Patrick's face pales when we turn to the source of the new voice.

Jarred.

CHAPTER 10
JARRED

I don't think I've ever been this angry in my life.

I was livid when I realized that my counselors were throwing a party after curfew. It's not even that they were out here in the first place—kids are going to be kids—but I grew furious when I noticed they were drinking, even though most of them are of age. What if the campers saw them? What kind of example would that send to impressionable children? Regardless, I was prepared to just walk away, call it a fluke, and readdress the rules with them tomorrow like a calm and rational adult.

I'm not calm and rational any more. Not after what I just witnessed.

Patrick had his hands on Noah. He had his lips pressed against his. He had his body so close that all it would take was a little gust of wind and they would be on top of each other. I don't know what the sudden rush of emotions is that I'm feeling. Anger, sure. Frustration? Of course. But the other one…

"What's happening here?" I bark, breaking my train of thought. My eyes zero in on something that rests on the boulder right next to them and my nose keys in on the scent that lingers in the air. "Is that marijuana?"

Patrick, still caught up in his shock, doesn't move, but Noah springs into action. He schools his surprised face and steps in front of Patrick. "It's mine."

I rub at my temples and growl. "Of course, it all comes back to you."

Noah pinches his face in anger and opens his mouth to say something, but Patrick beats him to it. "Mr. Walker, I'm so sorry—"

"I don't want to hear shit from you!" I yell, pointing a trembling finger at him. I'm shocked by my own words. I *never* curse, not out of anger, and especially not at my counselors, but I can't help it. I march up to Patrick, grab his shoulders, and spin him in the direction of where the party is taking place. "Tell the rest of them to clear out before I fire their asses! Noah, come with me!"

I start walking without looking back, going deeper and deeper into the woods as my fury only increases. What would have happened if I hadn't gotten here? Would Patrick have unzipped Noah's pants and kissed something else? Would they have been caught, pants around their ankles as Noah…

No, I can't think of that. Noah grabs my arm when we've walked for a few minutes in fuming silence. He forces me to stop and steps in front of me. "What the hell? You didn't have to yell at him like that!"

"That's what you're worried about?" I ask, throwing my hands in the air in frustration. "Patrick's fucking feelings?"

He takes a step back and his eyes narrow at me. He shakes his head and looks me up and down in confusion. "What's gotten into you?"

"You two were kissing."

"It was just—Wait." His jaw drops and he has the audacity to laugh as he looks back in the direction we came. "*That's* why you're pissed? Because we were kissing?"

I didn't mean to say that, but now that I have, I can't take it back. "It's wrong!"

He shakes his head and steps to me, tipping his head to the side with a cocky smirk. "Is it wrong because we're both guys or because it wasn't you?"

He's caught me. Fuck. I…No. It's wrong because they're both guys. It's wrong because it's a sin. It's wrong because counselors aren't supposed to be fraternizing. It's wrong for so many fucked up reasons and none of them center around my being jealous of Patrick fucking Cooper.

But that's not what I say. In my anger, in my frustration, in my lack of any rational thought, I say something entirely different. "Did you like it?"

He shrugs. "It was a kiss."

"That's not an answer."

"Are you asking if it felt the way it did when I kissed you?" he asks, reaching for my hand, that stupid half-smirk still on his lips as he hooks our pinkies together. "No, it didn't but you know that. Tell me, Jarred. Why are you really angry?"

"I didn't..." I try to swallow down my words, but I can't. It's like Noah has some sort of power over me that makes me want to spill all my secrets. It's like he's been sent by God to test me, and I keep repeatedly failing. "I didn't like his hands on you."

He takes a slow step forward and gently wraps his hands around my neck. "Do something about it then."

And this time, it's me who crashes my lips against his.

I swallow down his surprised yelp as my hands encircle his waist. I back him up until he's pressed against the tree and I'm grinding against him. It's like I can't control myself. He just has this air of aloofness, this mysterious anger that gets to me, this ability to make all my thoughts muddle together until I can't think straight. He tastes like alcohol and smoke and sex and I can't get enough of it.

"Fuck, babe," he groans, running his hands up and down my back as he tugs on my bottom lip. "Your lips. I could fucking do this all day."

I shush him as I dive down for another kiss. "Don't talk."

"What? If I don't talk you can just magically forget I'm not a woman?" he asks, but it's with no malice, almost as if he's taunting me. He brings one of my hands down to his crotch and I moan when I feel him hard underneath me. "What about this? Come on, Jarred. Give it a squeeze."

I do. I squeeze him hard and all the blood in my body shoots down to my cock. He's so long, so thick, so incredibly molded that I want to get down on my knees for a better look.

"That's right. You love a good cock in your hand. Look at you, you're even fucking drooling," he mumbles against my lips, rubbing his cock against my hand. He reaches for me and pulls back when he palms my crotch. "What's this?"

"It's…"

"Stop me if you don't want this," he says quietly, reaching for my belt. When I don't say anything, he carefully undoes it, pulling down my boxers along with my pants until they're hugging the middle of my thighs. His eyes widen and his jaw drops, but there's a twinkle of something in his hazel eyes as he looks at my cock. "What do we have here?"

The metal wrapped around my cock is painful. The cage digs into my erection, preventing me from getting fully hard, and I wince when he runs his fingers down the silver ridges until he reaches my inflamed balls.

"Oh, Jarred…" he says softly, tracing his finger up and down my cock cage as he looks up at me with sympathy. "Babe, what did you do to yourself?"

It's embarrassing. I didn't think that this would happen tonight. I hadn't been thinking when I had put the cage on. I had been plagued with thoughts of Noah, so many fucking thoughts, and I just wanted them to go away. I wanted to punish myself for thinking about him in that way. I was willing to do anything. So, I went through my old belongings and brought out something I hadn't had to use in years.

"I couldn't stop thinking of you," I admit, shuddering when he encircles the cock cage and gives it a light tug. "I wanted to stop thinking of you."

"Where's the key?" he questions. When I don't respond, his eyes narrow and his lips set in a firm line. "Give me the key, Jarred."

I shake my head. "It's in my cabin."

He lets out a deep breath, still lightly stroking me through the cage. "Does it hurt?"

"Yes."

"Do you want me to make it better?" he asks, falling to his knees in front of me. He places a gentle kiss against the head of the cage. "I can make it all better, babe."

I should say no. The whole reason for the cage was to prevent anything like this from happening. I jerked off to him once and, although the blinding pleasure was enough to satisfy me, the guilt that followed paralyzed me.

But I'm only a man. I'm only human, and Noah is on his knees for me, kissing around the cage, his mouth open and eager for me. "Please."

He smiles up at me tenderly as he licks one long stripe down the cage, his tongue twirling around when he reaches my balls. Although he can't fully get to my cock, he tries his hardest, worming his tongue in between the metal bars to lick at my swollen head.

"I think I can make you come like this," he says when he pulls back, a wicked grin on his lips as he teases the back of my balls. "I think you're so worked up that it won't take much, will it?"

I shake my head, wishing that he could put his lips back on me, and put me out of my misery. "No."

"No, it won't take much, or no you don't want to come?" he teases, flicking his tongue against my sac.

"Don't stop," I beg, pushing my hips out so the cage rubs up against his cheek. He chuckles to himself before swallowing me whole and even through the metal, I can feel his hot tongue sliding across my skin.

It's all a blur of pleasure and sin and vice as he expertly works me in his mouth. He gets me all the way to the back of his throat like the cage doesn't bother him at all. He looks up at me as he sucks two fingers into his mouth and doesn't break eye contact as he slides them in between my crease and gently circles my hole.

I've always imagined going there. I've always pictured what something would feel like pressed against my opening. I never thought it was possible, but I come, and I come *hard*. I unleash myself with a shout, my come overflowing the cage and dripping onto the ground beneath us. Noah's greedy as he laps it all up, sucking me clean.

When he stands, he presses a gentle kiss against my lips and helps me tuck myself back in. He reaches one hand up to rub the back of my neck in a soothing motion that makes me press my forehead against his.

"Next time, that's happening without the cock cage," he says, kissing my temple. "No matter how pretty you look in it."

That brings a deep hit of reality, and the panic sets in. "This can't happen again."

"Say that again but louder," he laughs, still kissing all over my face.

"So, you and Patrick?" I ask, feeling the stupid need to quell my curiosity, to wonder if he would have done this to that guy if I hadn't interrupted them, to know if he was willing to sin with anyone else.

He gently cups my face in his hands, his eyes so fucking tender it makes my heart crack. "There is no me and Patrick."

"Um, good," I cough, suddenly feeling the need for some space. No. That's wrong. I don't need or want space, but I have to put it between us. I step back and rub my hand down the wrinkles on my shirt. "I should go."

"Hey, stop," he says, grabbing onto my elbow as I try to walk away from him. "We didn't do anything wrong."

"Yes. Yes, we did," I say, admitting my shame, feeling as if God won't be able to forgive this. "It was dirty and immoral and—"

"Gay," he deadpans, a sudden fury in his eyes as he spits out the word. "The word you're looking for is gay."

"It's a sin—"

"I'll stop you right there. I don't want to hear it," he snaps, holding his hand up in the air. He looks at me, something pleading in his gaze before dropping his hand with a sigh. He scrunches the top of his beanie and curses, kicking at the ground as he walks back away from me. "Sorry about the weed."

And like a coward, I watch him walk away. I watch him slip out of my reach, both physically and emotionally. I want Noah. If tonight has made anything clear, it's that I can't help myself when I'm around him, but I know I have to be strong. My resolve must bend, and my will must not suffer.

Even if he just gave me the best orgasm of my life.

CHAPTER 11
NOAH

Finally, I get to do something I like for a change.

As I glide my paintbrush over the blank canvas, a serene sense of peace fills me. I've always been able to get lost in my art, lost in the way each stroke builds to something unseen and unknown until it develops in front of me.

Week three of camp is here and that means that all the elective activities have started. Last week, all the kids were grouped together in everything we did, but now they have the chance to branch out into the individual areas they like. I break my eyes away from my canvas, wipe my hands on the rag on my shoulder, and walk around the room. Some of these kids are really good and others...they could use a little practice, but we have all summer for that.

Fuck, since when have I started looking forward to the rest of the summer?

"That's great..." I blank on the girl's name whose art I'm checking out. "...kid. Keep going."

I make my way to the back of the studio so I can watch everyone paint at once when Jarred walks in. Immediately, I tense.

He's been keeping his distance since I gave him head in the woods, much like he had before then, but I've tried to not let it bother me. Sure, maybe I feel a twinge of hurt when he sees me walking and turns in the opposite direction. Yeah, maybe I feel a bit cheap and used when he won't even look me in the eyes and insist that Kendall handle the communication between us. But the metaphorical ball is in his court. If he wants me, he needs to do something about it. I begged for my parents' attention all my life, and I'm not about to go through that again.

Jarred stops right behind me, smiling at one of the kids before turning to me. "How is everything?"

I suck at my front teeth and shrug. "Good."

"Well, that's…" He trips over his words as he clears his throat, red splotching his neck as he nods. "…that's good. Keep going."

He leaves just like that with a little awkward parting exchange, and I let out a breath I didn't know I was holding. Thankfully, I can't stew on what just happened when Ian comes up to me. "Hey, Noah?"

"What's up?"

"Are you sure I can't call my parents?" he asks, looking sheepishly over at his terrible-looking painting of an apple. "It's important."

"Dude, I've told you five times already, no," I groan. "Write them a letter and mail it to them."

He crosses his arms over his chest and pouts. "I have, but they haven't responded yet."

"That's because this isn't Facebook Messenger." I roll my eyes and walk with him back to his canvas. "It'll take a bit for them to get back to you."

"If they ever do…" he mumbles under his breath, but I catch it. He sinks into his seat and hangs his head down, not even looking at his canvas as he lifts his brush and restarts his painting.

"Is everything okay, Ian?" I ask, actually fucking concerned for once. I sigh to myself for being a dick and pull out a seat next to him, careful not to speak too loudly in front of the other campers. "What's up?"

"I'm fine," he says stubbornly, not meeting my eyes, but the nervous little twitch in his nose makes me not believe that shit at all. He obviously doesn't want to talk about it, and I'm not going to push, but I'm going to keep an eye on him from now on.

The rest of the art session goes by well. I walk around and give some critiques in areas kids could improve, and some helpful tips when they ask for them, and I actually feel good about myself as I clean up the art room. When the door opens and closes, I don't turn around because I have a feeling I know who it is. Jarred's going to have to do better than some half-assed conversation if he wants to get with me. I turn around to tell him just that and blink when I see it's Patrick.

He's also been keeping his distance since that night in the woods. I'm still not too sure why he kissed me, but it really wasn't a big deal to me. I was flattered, not really interested in anything else, but flattered, nonetheless.

I'm a very upfront person. If there's something that needs to be talked about, I don't hold back. Sure, it's gotten me an ass-whooping from my parents in the past, but it's a habit I can't break. But I resolve to be patient as Patrick moves from one foot to the other and stares at me.

Obviously, I'm going to have to go first.

"How did your guitar lessons go?" I ask as I dip a bundle of brushes in water. I never pegged Patrick as a guitar player, but I overheard one of his lessons, and he's actually good.

"Good," he says. He bites his lip nervously as he fidgets. "Do you need any help?"

"I'll take it," I say with a shrug. "The canvases get stacked against that wall. Mine gets locked up in the cabinet."

We quietly clean up the art studio in relative peace, but I don't miss the way he glances over in my direction every now and then. The air is stifling with uncomfortable tension that I don't like. Sometimes, he opens his mouth as if he's going to say something, but then snaps it shut a second later. Finally, I decide that I have to be the one to start.

"We should talk."

He doesn't look up at me or stop what he's doing, sorting through the different color tubes by the canvases. "About what?"

"Come on. Don't play like that," I say, hating that everyone lately likes to bury their heads in the sand. Apparently, it's unique to this camp. "The kiss."

The clattering of easels makes me jump as Patrick turns on his heels to face me. His face is red with mortification and his fingers fidget as he awkwardly tries to fix his mess. "Noah, I'm so sorry. I should have asked you before I did that. I didn't get your consent and that was wrong."

"Man, it's okay. Don't sweat it," I say, trying to appease him. I head over to help him pick up what he knocked down, and I don't have the heart to tell him he broke one of the easels. "You're right that consent is important, but you didn't make me uncomfortable. I just wanna know what it was about."

"I wanted to see if I was attracted to you...like that."

I raise my pierced brow. "And?"

"Nothing."

"Ouch."

"Sorry."

"No, I'm just messing with you," I laugh, rubbing at his back to assure him. "I'm glad I could clear some things up."

"It didn't, actually," he confesses, huffing as he sits down on a stool. "It made it worse."

I teeter on my heels. On one hand, he looks like he doesn't want anything to do with this conversation. Patrick is skittish by nature, but he looks full-on ready to bolt. On the other hand, he's the closest thing I have to a friend here, so I don't want something as simple as a kiss to mess with that. "Want to talk about it?"

"I don't...like I don't get..." He gulps audibly as he gingerly points to his crotch. "...erect."

I scrunch my nose in confusion. "What do you mean?"

"For anything," he says, flustered. "I mean, sometimes I'll wake up with an erection—"

"Hard on, Patrick," I snort. "Just call it a hard-on."

"Yeah, well, *that*." He chews on the inside of his cheek as his pale cheeks flush. "I really like Kendall."

"I noticed." I think we all noticed. Patrick gets all starry-eyed when she's around. It's kind of adorable the way he follows her like a puppy, doing anything she asks, and always being available to her. It's cute, actually. Borderline creepy, but still.

"And I really like you too."

I puff out my chest in pride. What? I'm only human. "Well, thanks."

"But I'm not sexually attracted to either of you. I've never really been sexually attracted to anybody. This—" He gestures at my body, making a point to hover specifically over my hips. "—does nothing for me."

I sit on the stool beside him, resting my elbows on my knees as I try to get him to make eye contact with me. "That bothers you?"

"Yeah, it's not normal. I'm young and healthy. I should be able to feel...*aroused*, right?" he asks.

That's a good question. I've never really had to deal with not feeling turned on. Fuck, if anything, I get turned on too easily. Even though my body has aggressively and stubbornly insisted that Jarred's dick is the only one we want to suck, I will admit that I chubbed up a bit when Patrick kissed me. I've never had to deal with wondering if I was attracted to somebody, it's just always been guaranteed.

This makes me feel a little bit bad for Patrick. I don't pity him, nowhere near that. It's just obvious that he's struggling with this and, at twenty-one, he must be so frustrated to not know this part of him.

"I don't know, man. There are a lot of colors in the rainbow," I explain. "Did you ever consider if you were asexual?"

He looks up at me with wide eyes that hide behind his thick glasses. "What's that?"

"It's basically what you're describing, I think? I'm not an expert, but maybe you're even demi?" I offer. I'm not an expert on all matters LGBTQIA+ but what he's describing sounds close to something I've heard about before. There are people out there who feel emotional love while not being interested in sex. It's a thing. And if it's a thing to somebody, it's valid and real. "You should read up on it, but you shouldn't let it bother you."

He snorts, and it's only now that I realize he's started to cry. "Why not?"

"Because you're *you*," I say, scooting closer to him so I can throw my arm over his thin shoulders. "You are who you are and there's nothing wrong or abnormal about it. If you're not ready to label it, you don't have to."

His eyes peer up at me as he snuggles closer to my side. "You really think so?"

"Oh, one hundred percent. I know it's easier said than done, but there's nothing wrong with you," I say with a smile, squeezing him tight against me. "If you ever want to talk about it more, or even experiment, I'm here for you."

And I never expected that would happen. I never thought that I'd actually find a friend in this place. Patrick and I are so insanely different, but I can't deny the urge to protect him and make sure he's okay.

He sniffles as he wipes his nose with the back of his hand. "Thanks, Noah."

"Anytime."

We both get up at the same time and go back to our respective corners to finish up cleaning. After a minute, he asks. "What are your plans for the rest of the day?"

Despite not having any service, I check my phone and curse. "Fuck. I have van duty in a few minutes."

"I can finish up here if you have to go," Patrick offers, seeing that the only thing we really have left to do is hang the aprons. "I have ministry group at five, so I have time."

"Thanks and good luck." I go to leave but something stops me. I've managed to keep it in the back of my head this last week, but after our impromptu therapy session, my insecurities have been brought to the forefront. "Can I ask you something?"

"After what I told you?" he asks with a laugh. "Anything."

I bite my bottom lip painfully. I really don't want to ask, but I need to know. "Do you think God is okay with the fact that you kissed me?"

To my question, his eyes widen. Fuck, I knew that was a bad idea. It's just…Jarred's fucked with my head.

I want him. I want him so fucking much, but he has it in his head that wanting me back is wrong. It's not like my parents didn't instill the same mentality in me, but I've been out in the world now. I know that there's nothing wrong with being gay, straight, pan, bi—however you identify—but Jarred hasn't gotten that memo.

Patrick shuffles on his feet as he lets out a weak chuckle. "Maybe he's not like *thrilled* about it, but He loves us all, doesn't he?"

"Yeah," I say slowly, not entirely sure whether I like that answer. "I guess he does."

CHAPTER 12
JARRED

"Jarred, can I talk to you for a second?"

I stop in my tracks as Father Matteo steps in front of me. We've just finished another round of last-minute confession, and I'm running late. Regardless, I turn to him with a smile as I subtly check my watch. "Of course."

Father Matteo smiles kindly at me. "It's not that I'm not here for you, or that you're a nuisance, but I've noticed you've been asking for confession a lot lately."

I resist the urge to wince and chuckle. "I just want to be absolved for my sins. Father."

"And I get that. We all seek His forgiveness, but I've known you for years and you've never come this much," he says. He pauses, and I can only assume he's giving me a second to fill in the blanks he's missing, but I don't. When I refuse to speak, he sighs. "Is there anything you'd like to talk about?"

There are several things I'd like to talk about.

I'd like to talk about the fact that Noah Scott has messed with my head. I want to tell Father Matteo that I can't stop thinking about Noah. I can't stop thinking about the way his tongue licked at the metal ridges of my cock cage. I can't stop thinking about the way his piercing felt against my lips when he kissed me. I can't stop thinking about wanting *more*.

Not only that, but I want to talk about how *obsessed* I am with this nineteen-year-old kid.

It's not even that I'm attracted to him physically, it's more than that. In my quest to avoid him, I've become finely tuned with his routine and the people he hangs around. I've seen how kind he is to Kendall, who can sometimes be a bit too much. I've seen how compassionate he is with Patrick, who needs a few lessons on social cues. I've witnessed the aftermath of his rage after someone insulted his friend. I've seen how loyal he can be, even knowing he might get fired for his actions.

Noah Scott is beautiful and mysterious. He carries his anger like a weapon to wield, and it's stunning when the fight is relinquished, and you get to see all of him. The way he talks to me...so sweet, so kind, so *dirty* makes my insides curl.

I want to tell Father Matteo that I want to spend hours talking with Noah. I want to figure out where all that anger comes from. I want to know everything about him. I want to be the one he drops those shields for after he holds me close to him and tells me how perfect I am.

I wish I could tell Father Matteo these things, but I can't. It's bad enough that I'm already thinking of it. When it's spoken into truth, that's when it becomes a true sin.

"No."

He doesn't look convinced. "If you're sure…"

"Positive," I beam back, smiling widely to cover up the fact that I've started to sweat. "I actually have to go. I wish I could stay and chat."

"Of course, I understand." He eyes me wearily, maybe hoping that I'll give him *something*, but I don't. He sighs and gives me the sign of the cross. "I'll see you at mass tomorrow."

I leave the chapel before Father Matteo can try to drag anything else out of me. Instead of making my way straight through to the van, I bypass that route and head over to the dance studio. The music is thumping loudly on the other side of the door when I reach it, so I let myself in. Kendall's standing in the center of the class, hair in two pigtails as she tries to teach the kids to do a box step. I smile tenderly at how uncoordinated they all look, like little baby deer trying to find their footing.

"Hey, Kendall?"

"Mr. Walker! Kids, keep practicing. I'll be right back." She bounces toward me with all that great enthusiasm. "What's up?"

"Just Jarred," I say, reminding her that *Mr. Walker* is the name of my father, not me. "I have to go into town to pick up some things. Keep an eye out on the camp when you're done?"

Her face brightens as she brings her hands to her chest. "Oh my! Absolutely! Thank you so much for trusting me!"

"Just make sure nothing burns down," I chuckle, watching as she nearly fans herself to stay calm. "Father Matteo is in the chapel if you need anything."

Technically he's qualified to run the camp too, but I want to give Kendall a bit of leadership training. She's been an excellent bunk leader, and I can see that she has a future in this industry if she ever chooses to go down this path. If she wanted a job here year-round, I'd give it to her in a heartbeat.

Kendall is one of the good kids. She's smart, sweet, and attentive. She's nothing but kindness and rainbows and promises for a happy future.

Unlike—

"Is there anything else you need?"

I shake myself out of my own head. Kendall's got her brows pinched in worry as she looks at me. I quickly school my features and smile. "No. I'll let you know when I'm back."

She nods happily and goes back to her instruction, praising one particular student even though they've managed to kick their partner in the shins. I exit the studio after that, not wanting to witness any more painful accidents.

I don't like leaving the camp at all if I can help it, but I'm planning a barbecue after mass tomorrow, and need to pick up some last-minute things. I run through the list in my head as I make my way to the edge of the camp where we park the vans. I'm not looking where I'm going and nearly run into the counselor until a firm hand stops me.

"Oh, I'm sorry. I—What are you doing here?"

Noah furrows his brows in confusion as he smokes his cigarette. Leaning against the edge of the van, his shaggy hair hidden under his beanie, his *Camp Trinity* T-shirt tight on his body, he looks so at ease. So opposite of the way I'm feeling. I look down at the spot where his hand is touching me and I jump back.

"It's my turn on van duty," he says casually, taking another drag of his cigarette as he reaches into the van for the schedule. "What? You're the one that made it."

"I...I didn't see that," I say, stuttering through my words as I look at the schedule and take a step back.

He raises his brows and deadpans me with a bored look. "Is this going to be a problem?"

I look back over my shoulder at the camp. Since it's on the schedule, everybody else who's licensed to drive the van is already busy. I look back at Noah and his apathetic expression. Why is it that he always needs to look so...edible? Even with his grumpy mood and his sour face, he's still one of the most stunning things I've seen.

The light afternoon humidity makes his shirt stick to his skin, showcasing that lithe body I've felt against mine. His nose piercings glitter when the sunlight hits them just right. His lip piercing moves and jostles as he tugs on his bottom lip.

"I guess it's not," I say, handing him back the schedule. "A problem, I mean. No, it's not a problem."

He nods as he snorts to himself and puts out his cigarette, crunching it under his boot before hopping into the van. "Let's go then."

I gulp audibly as I go to the passenger side. I enter slowly, almost cautiously, and he doesn't waste any time taking off. He asks where we're going, and I give him a mumbled response. After a few minutes, I can't bear to sit in silence any longer. We're an hour away from the closest little mountain town, and I'm going to go crazy if I can't talk.

But it's not just that. Noah looks so...*aloof*. Cool and distant in the worst way. I told myself that it was best to keep some distance from him, but I want to know him. The craving, the itch, the unrelenting need to be inside that fascinating mind is overwhelming.

"So," I cough, adjusting the collar of my polo just to give my hands something to do. "You go to UNC?"

He turns in my direction with a pinched look on his face. Those hazel eyes stare at me for far too long, so long that I feel like any longer and I might launch myself across the console at him. He's appraising me curiously, searching for something in my expression, and I'm not quite sure what it is. After a beat, he gives the most half-assed smile I've ever seen. "Yeah."

"What are you majoring in?" I ask.

Once again, he waits. He seems to relax after a second and this time, his smile is more sincere. "Graphic Design."

"Why that?"

"I like art, but I know I'd never make it as an artist. Graphic design lets me have some job security while also being creative," he admits, carefully turning on the blinker as he weaves through the tight winding mountain roads. "What about you? What made you want to start Camp Trinity?"

I sink into my seat and think my answer through. "I've always had a special relationship with God, and I wanted to spread His word to the new generation. Catholics are known for being stuffy, and I wanted to give kids a religious experience that was not only fun but also meaningful."

His nose does a funny little twitch, and he quickly glances at me. "Really?"

"Really," I say, wrinkling my own nose. "Why?"

He shrugs and lets out a deep sigh. "That sounded rehearsed."

How is it that he always sees right through me? Yes, I wanted to start Camp Trinity for all the reasons I told him, but it's more than that. I wanted it because the guilt...the guilt of wanting something I couldn't have became so strong. I thought that maybe if I started this camp for Him, everything would be better. I'd have a life mission I could focus on and devote all my energy to.

But that didn't stop the thoughts. It didn't stop the cravings. It didn't stop my *wants*.

But I don't tell him that. Instead, I change the subject. "Are you liking the camp any better than when you first started?"

His tongue flicks out against his piercing as he exhales deeply. "It's growing on me. It's chiller than I thought it would be."

"I told you if you gave it a chance, you'd like it."

"Well, there are several things to like about it."

I don't miss the way his eyes track every corner of my face. I think it's supposed to be subtle, but it's so loud in the confines of this car. Is he saying that I'm one of the things he likes about camp? How can it be when I've been nothing but terrible to him?

Is it because he feels what I feel too? This all-consuming, hungry, desperate need to be with him?

"Maybe we should just drive in silence," I whisper, looking away from him and out the window. He doesn't say anything else, and I don't know if I'm grateful for that.

The drive feels longer than it should with the stifling silence, and I practically jump out of the car while it's still moving to get away from it. Noah doesn't follow me, and I look back to see that he's lighting another cigarette, perched on the hood of the van. Christ, how is it possible that he makes something so disgusting look so good?

I shake my head and walk into the store. I hate to admit that I linger a bit, browsing each aisle when I already know what it is I want. I just need to get away from him. He's sin and temptation wrapped up in a perfectly delicious package, and I don't know how much longer I can hold out.

I realize that after fifteen minutes, I've stalled for too long. As I check out, I feel a little bad about ditching Noah but that goes away the second I walk out of the store. I nearly drop the paper bags as a beautiful woman—tall, blonde, leggy—runs her hand up and down his arm, bringing her chest close to him as she flutters her eyelashes.

Once again, the foreign feeling of rage crashes through me. It's so odd and disconcerting. I'm not a man that feels rage. I'm a man of patience and forgiveness, but the sight of that blonde tramp with her hands all over Noah sets me over the edge. It gets even worse when he chuckles at something she says and tucks a strand of hair behind her ear.

"Get in the van, Noah," I bark, shoving the bags in his unprepared hands. He fumbles for a bit, nearly dropping them. When he doesn't move, I grab him by his arm and haul him away from the woman, basically throwing him into the van. "Let's go!"

The blonde goes to say something, but one look from me shuts her up. I march to the other side of the van and rip the door open. Noah looks between me and the woman, but he makes the smart choice when he drops the bags in the backseat and gets in the van.

"What the fuck?" he asks as he starts the van. "What was that about?"

"What?" I snap.

"*Get in the van, Noah.* That's the second fucking time you've lost your cool with me. Why is that?"

I try to bite my tongue. *Because she was beautiful. Because you were touching her. Because you can't touch anybody else but me.* "Promiscuity is frowned upon by God."

"The girl? Seriously?" he says, groaning loudly as he white knuckles the steering wheel. "Fuck, Jarred. We were just talking."

"She was flirting with you."

"And?" he bites, throwing me a glare as we start our ascent up the mountain. "You've made it loud and clear that you want nothing to do with me."

I grip the edges of my seat tightly. *But I do want you. I want to kiss you. I want to feel you. I want to lick every inch of your skin.* "Noah, we just can't. It's not right."

"Because of God," he scoffs angrily. "What bullshit!"

"It's not bullshit!"

"Yes, it is!" he shouts, slamming one hand on the steering wheel. He's focusing on the road, but the furious clench in his jaw combats any glare he could give me. "You're a grown man! You can make your own decisions without having to consult God every point two seconds! What do *you* fucking want?"

"You!"

The words are out of my mouth before I can think better of it. *Him. Noah. That's what I want. I want to quell this dirty need within me. I want to experience the perverse pleasure of being with him. I want him more than I've ever wanted anybody else and, God forgive me, I can't help it anymore.*

"Pull over."

His eyes widen and his jaw drops. All of his beautiful rage is gone. "What?"

I bite my bottom lip until I can feel the sharp sting of pain. "I said, *pull over.*"

He gives me a questioning look but does what I say. Luckily, we're in a flat area of the mountain—remote and coated with nothing but wilderness—so we're in no danger of getting hit by a car or driving off the side of a cliff.

When he brings the van to a full stop, he turns fully to me. His chest is still heaving, and he's looking at me expectantly. Right. I told him to pull over, but I hadn't thought this through. Now that we're here—alone—I can finally give into my deafening and crippling urge.

I launch myself over the console, hands reaching for his cheeks as I slam my lips against his. I take him by surprise, so it takes him a second to reciprocate but when he does, my insides curl.

His tongue curls around the corners of my mouth, his teeth clash with mine, and a husky groan escapes him when I rip off his beanie and dig my hands into his hair.

"You just can't help it, can you?" he breathes in between kisses, hands wrapped around my throat as he pulls me closer to him, nearly bringing me over to his seat. "You want me that badly."

"Yes," I say wantonly. There's no use denying it now. I might regret this later but at this moment, all I want is to get lost in the pure bliss I know he can deliver.

He brings his mouth down on mine again as he reaches for my pants. "I want to suck on you until you cream in my mouth."

His foul mouth makes my blood boil in pure unadulterated lust. I want him to keep talking to me like that. I want the filthiest of words to pour out of those beautifully pierced lips.

He gets my pants open, and I lift up to help him get my boxers over my ass. Once my cage-covered cock is exposed, those hazel eyes flick back up to me, filled with such raw hunger. "Do you have the key this time?"

I nod. After the other night, the pain I felt before he put me out of my misery, I decided it would be safer to keep the key on me. And maybe a little part of myself that I don't want to own up to knew this would happen again. Unavoidable. Inevitable. Undeniable. "Yes."

With shaky hands, I reach for the key ring hooked to my belt. I fumble as I isolate the key to the cage, and it's out of my hands as soon as he sees which one it is. When he unlocks the cage, my dick must double in size. I look down and see how angry it is, how red it appears, and how thick and prominent the veins are that wrap around and stop right at the head.

"What a beautiful cock, babe," he purrs, running one finger up and down my length, teasing me with touches so light I can barely feel them. "Unlike you, it knows what it wants."

I swallow back my retort when he swallows me in one go. His mouth is hot and ready, sliding down my length and taking me all the way to the hilt. I choke on a moan when he comes back up, swirling his tongue around my dick until he reaches the head and gives me one hard suck.

"Noah…" I mumble, drunk on the lust and the sin and the danger. "You're so good at this."

He gives the head one gentle kiss. "Do you trust me?"

"Yes." With my body I do. I trust that anything he does to me will feel good, feel euphoric, feel like the best fucking thing in the world.

He licks his lips as he moves away from me and chuckles at my whine when he gets out of my reach. "Take your pants off."

I hate how quickly I rush to comply. It's a bit of a tight stretch, undressing in a cramped van, but the promise of the ending has me ripping them off faster than humanly possible.

"Turn yourself toward me."

I'm not quite sure what he's asking for, so I angle myself so that my back is pressed against the closed door and my legs drape over the console. He seems to be pleased with the position when he scooches forward and runs his hands down my thighs. "Gorgeous. So fucking gorgeous. Okay. If I do anything you don't like, you have to say something."

I nod, but I doubt there's anything this man can do to me that I won't enjoy. He leans forward as much as he can, latching his hands onto the back of my thighs, and pushing them up until they hit my chest. I feel so exposed in the position that a hot flush sears through me, but it only makes me hotter and more desperate.

He gently fondles my ass, squeezing my cheeks in his large hands as he pulls them apart and stares at my hole. "How pretty and pink, looks like it's going to be a tight squeeze."

"Are you going to fuck me?" I squeak out, and I hate how weak I sound at this moment.

"No, not yet." He hums to himself as he traces his finger down my crease. "Have you ever had any fingers up here?"

I gulp. "No."

He nods pensively. I'm entirely unprepared and thoroughly scandalized when he bends down and licks one single stripe up my crack, only stopping momentarily to flutter his tongue against my hole. I throw back my head with a moan. He pulls my cheeks farther apart, teasing at my rim, poking and prodding until I can feel him *inside* me.

I look down just as he looks up. He pulls back for a moment and brings two fingers up to his mouth, sucking and licking them obscenely as his eyes continue to bore into mine. He doesn't take his eyes off me as his fingers disappear from my view, and my breath hitches when I feel them pressing against my hole.

"Deep breath for me, babe," he whispers, squeezing the inside of my thigh when I wince. "Just let me in."

I do, letting out a deep breath that's paired with a moan as he breeches me.

"How does it feel?"

"Like I can feel you everywhere," I say, trembling and arching my back when he works them deeper into me.

"That's right. Feel me deep inside you. Feel me stuffing you with my fingers," he says, a cocky smirk on his lips when I cry out as he scissors his fingers inside me. "Let me finger fuck you until you come."

"Okay—*Fuck!*" I shout, blessed with nothing but bright zaps of pleasure when he reaches somewhere deep inside me. "Noah!"

"There it is," he coos. "I love it when you scream my name."

And that's all I can do. Just scream his name, whine for him, beg him to keep fucking me with his fingers. He takes me back down the back of his throat, and I see stars. The obscenely filthy sound of his fingers fucking my ass rings through the van as he brings me closer and closer to ecstasy. Nothing has ever felt this good. Nothing has ever lit me up like this. Nothing has ever made me feel so…

"Noah!" I shout, unable to control myself as I come down his throat, breathing out on a long shaky exhale. "Yes!"

Noah pulls back and looks thoroughly satisfied with himself. I whimper when he pulls his fingers out of me, already feeling the phantom loss and the deep ache in my ass.

He crawls over the console and kisses me, and it's so much gentler than it was before. I think it's meant to comfort me, meant to reassure me, and meant to make me forget what a horrible idea this was.

Forgive me, Father.

I break away from him, panting against his lips. "Noah—"

"I'm keeping the cage," he says, nuzzling his nose against mine. "You don't have to punish yourself for wanting this."

"But I do."

Oh, how I wish that didn't have to be true. I wish that I could accept this side of myself. I wish that I could live as boldly and freely as he does. I wish that the circumstance was different, and I could enjoy this post-orgasmic haze, but I can't.

Pain. Numbness.

"Again. Do it again until you feel His forgiveness."

Disappointment flashes through those pretty hazel eyes. For a moment, Noah looks as young as he is, but that's quickly schooled when he pulls away from me. He gets back into his seat as I awkwardly fumble for my pants. He grips the steering wheel and drops his head against it, rubbing his forehead back and forth against the wheel before turning to me.

"Jarred…that's enough. I'm not going to play this game with you," he says, firmly and with a conviction I wish I could have. "If you want this to go any further between us, the God talk has to stop. I'm done hearing about how wrong I am. If we're going to do this, it's enough."

I pause halfway through buckling my belt. "I—"

"No," he says as he starts the car. "I'll give you time to think about it."

He doesn't say anything else as he begins to drive back to camp.

That's fine by me because he's given me too much to think about. Do I want this to happen again? More than anything. Can it? It shouldn't.

But I can't deny how much I want this, how much it meant to me, and how desperately I need it to happen again.

It's so wrong, but God will just have to forgive me.

CHAPTER 13
JARRED

"Bryce? What are you doing here? Aren't you supposed to be teaching archery?"

I look up at Bryce with confusion. I haven't spoken to him since the day after he and Noah got into that fight.

Noah. Perfect, beautiful, angry Noah. Noah, who wants something from me I can't give him. Noah, whose temptation I can't resist.

I can't think about Noah right now, not when Bryce is in my office. It's not that I'm taking Noah's side, necessarily, but I can't help but be biased. I've always liked Bryce, but there's something about him this year that's hitting me the wrong way. Regardless, I smile at him as I wave him closer.

"Sheridan took over for a little bit," Bryce says, taking a seat across from me. "I was wondering if I could talk to you?"

"Of course. You know my door is always open. What's the matter?"

"It's about Noah."

I gulp, the tips of my ears burning. I cough lightly and try my best to school my features. "What about Noah?"

Bryce sits up straight, exuding a kind of cocky confidence I've never seen from him before. "I don't know if you've noticed it yet, but he doesn't really fit in here."

"The campers seem to like him just fine," I say, cocking my head to the side because I'm not too sure where this is going.

"Yeah but...he smokes weed," he rushes out, clenching his fists in his lap. "Did you know that?"

"No. That's news to me, but you know I can't do anything about that without proof," I lie. I've caught Noah smoking before, but I can't find it in me to care. When I caught him with marijuana that first night, it didn't even cross my mind to kick him out for it. Even though I would have kicked anyone else out for having drugs.

You're crossing so many lines for him...

"He smokes cigarettes."

"A nasty habit but perfectly legal."

"I mean just...look at him."

Yeah, that's the problem, Bryce. I *do* look at him. Too much. All the time. He's gorgeous with his shaggy black hair and too many piercings. I like that he picks at the black polish on his nails. I like that stupid beanie he insists on wearing every day. He's everything I never knew I wanted. He's temptation and sin and salvation and charity all together.

Bryce tenses. He obviously didn't think this was where the conversation was headed. His teeth are grit, his jaw is clenched, and he looks one second away from bursting. I lean forward, concern furrowing my brows. "What's this about?"

"He assaulted me," Bryce spits out. "He punched me."

"From what I gathered of that fight it was mutual," I say, trying to placate the situation. And it did seem to be an even fight, even with Joshua involved. Christ, Noah is so strong. He's...*stop it*. I tune back into Bryce. "We talked about this already, remember?"

Bryce, Joshua, and I did actually discuss this at length. The morning after the fight, I brought both of them into my office. I hate to admit that when I was concerned for Noah and treated his wounds, I just snapped at the other two men. Regardless, I thought this matter was settled and I have no idea why he's choosing to bring it up again.

"What do you want, Bryce?"

Bryce steels his eyes and raises his chin in defiance. "I want you to kick him out."

My eyes widen. Kicking Noah out...might be the solution I hadn't thought of. If I kicked him out, I wouldn't have to deal with the overbearing and consuming need to resist him. I would have him gone, out of my life, and I'd be in the clear.

But I'd never see him again. I'd never hear that raspy voice of his. I'd never feel the flutter in my stomach at his rare smiles. I'd never feel the way I feel now—anxiety and guilt aside—like someone's dragged me up into the air and let me free fall.

"Look, Noah might not be our...typical counselor, but he's here to stay unless he says otherwise. I suggest you two get along."

Bryce swallows harshly, his Adam's apple bobbing in frustration. He's seething as he stands, his chair screeching with the force of it. Nonetheless, his tone is polite but curt when he speaks. "Of course, sir. I'm sorry to bother you."

He leaves my office with tension tightening every inch of him. I should be worried about what he might do to Noah, but that's not what I'm thinking of.

I literally can't escape Noah. Even when he's not around, even when I manage to block him from my mind, he's right there.

I have to do something about this. Just...just one more sin. One more caving into devilry.

Just one more time and that's it.

CHAPTER 14
JARRED

My fingers are twitching at my sides, and it's suddenly hard to swallow.

My polo feels too tight on my skin, sticking to my damp chest as I approach the dock. Noah is sitting in the lifeguard's chair, head thrown back as his pale body takes in the sun's rays. He looks so freaking majestic like that—bare-chested with his pierced nipples glittering in the sunlight— put up on some pedestal like an altar for me to fall at my feet.

I swallow up my nerves as I approach him, forehead beaded with sweat and heart in my throat. "Noah?"

He notices me then. So very coolly, he leans forward and pushes down his sunglasses with his forefinger. "Yeah?"

"Can you…" I look around and see that all the kids and counselors by the lake are in the water. Regardless, I come closer as I keep my voice low. "Can you meet me at my cabin tonight?"

He cocks his head to the side in silence. For someone so young, he's mastered that cold aloofness of men twice his age. He bites down on his bottom lip before he nods. "Yeah. I just have to wait for Kendall to do her checks and I'll be there."

I give some sort of nod in confirmation and scramble after that. The day drags on at a snail's pace. My body twitches with every minute that passes. My body is on high alert. The anticipation bubbles and boils and pours over when it's finally nighttime. I spend my time waiting for him by cleaning up around my cabin—which is already spotless—and then...cleaning myself—which is slightly mortifying.

I have no idea what's going to happen when he gets here. Will he kiss me again? Lay me down on the bed and make me see stars? Will he tell me that he doesn't want to keep doing whatever it is we're doing? Is he going to make me beg him?

I'm impatient and agitated. By the time it hits curfew, I'm a nervous wreck. It doesn't get any better when a few minutes later, a knock on my door rings through the cabin. I audibly gulp and smooth down the wrinkles on my shirt, clearing my throat as I try to channel even an ounce of calmness.

I open the door and there's Noah. Perfect, mysterious, and cool Noah. He's dressed like everything I wouldn't have thought I wanted —black ripped jeans, a tight band t-shirt, and his duffel slung over his shoulder.

"Hey," he says, taking a final drag of his cigarette before he tosses it on the ground and stubs it with his boot.

I try to smile, but it probably comes out weird. "Hi."

"Cold feet?" he asks, gesturing at my fingers that twitch on the door handle.

I shake my head. "N—No."

"Then why don't you invite me in?"

I move to the side, giving him the room to come in. He does and sets his duffel bag on the floor. There are no pleasantries exchanged as he approaches me, reaching for my hips and pulling me against him. He's slightly shorter than I am, so I have to look down at him as he licks his lips.

"You look nervous," he accurately deduces.

"I am."

"Why?"

"I've never done this before."

"Done what?"

"Slept with a..." I can't finish my sentence. A part of me is mortified that I've gone through forty-five years of my life and haven't been

79

with a man. The other stronger part of me is ashamed to admit how long I've wanted this. A secret never to be spoken. A shame meant to be denied. A wish never meant to be granted.

But Noah doesn't want the *God talk*. I can appreciate that. He doesn't want whatever is going to happen to be tainted with ugliness, and I can relate. God doesn't live here anymore, not right now, and it's going to stay that way.

"I'll make it good for you," he says, fingering the bottom of my shirt as he slowly pushes it up to reveal my stomach. "I want to hear you tell me you want this."

I let out a shaky breath as he pulls my shirt over my head, my limbs numbly following along with his commands. His finger trails down my chest, pausing only to play with my chest hair. "W—Why?"

"Because I just do," he says with a shrug. He leans forward and kisses my pec, nipping at the skin before moving on to the next one. "I want your consent. I want to know that everything that's about to happen is something you actually want."

"I do want it. I want you, Noah," I rush out, sucking in a sharp breath when he reaches down to my stomach, and he plays with my happy trail. "What are you going to do to me?"

He brings his hand to the back of my neck and harshly yanks me forward. "I'm going to fuck you until you're screaming my name. I'm going to cram myself inside that hot hole until you're crying and begging me to come. I'm going to ruin you, Jarred."

And I want to be ruined by him. I want him to tear me apart and come on the pieces. I want him to demolish my sense and my reason. I want to be at his mercy and his alone.

I want him to fuck God right out of my head.

His gentle lips move against mine as he walks me backward toward the bed. The cabin is studio-style, so there's nowhere to run from him, not that I would want to. When the back of my legs hit the bed, he forces me down by my shoulders. He massages the tight muscles there, pulling away only to look at me, and the hunger in his eyes damn near obliterates me.

"You have no idea how much I've thought of this. I didn't think I'd ever get you like this." He lowers himself on his knees to undo my pants and slide them down my legs. "Now that I do, I'm going to take my time." He presses hot open-mouth kisses against my underwear-covered bulge before pulling them off too.

Once I'm fully naked—vulnerable and at his beck and call—he stands. As he pulls off his shirt, he rolls his lip piercing around his tongue and chuckles. "You're so fucking hot. I never thought daddies would do it for me but *damn*."

He shoves down his sweats, revealing a cock so gorgeous I might just beg him to gag me with it until I can't breathe. He's so much larger than I expected him to be, glistening at the tip, his veins running a deep blue, his—

Is that a fucking piercing at the base?

I drool.

"I brought something with me you might like."

I snap out of my daze and his answering smirk lets me know I've been caught. "What?"

He walks back to his duffel, giving me a fine view of his ass, and a peak at his hole as he bends down and rifles through his pack. He turns back to me and holds out something that makes my jaw drop.

"Is that a…" I gulp nervously, watching as he plays with the bright pink dildo in one hand and lube in another. I'm not even going to ask why Noah brought a fucking dildo to Catholic summer camp. It's beyond my reach at this point. "But I thought you were going to fuck me."

"Oh, I am. But I need to get you ready first, babe," he says, winking at me as he comes back to me. He drags the dildo against my cock, the fleshy texture giving me a delicious burst of friction that causes my eyes to flutter. "I need to stretch out that virgin hole before I get in there. Lay down. Legs spread."

My voice is caught in my throat as I follow his command. I'm so needy for him, panting as he slathers his fingers in lube first. He gently teases my rim, applying just the right amount of pressure as he slips two fingers into me. I groan at the sensation, his fingers scissoring me open, his whispered praises.

"Is this okay?" he asks, almost hesitantly, pressing a kiss to the base of my cock as he inserts another finger. I can't answer him. I'm so lost in bliss. All I do is nod dumbly, my hips canting in the air with a mind of their own. "Oh, you're doing so good, Jarred. Are you ready for more?"

"Y—Yes," I stutter, nodding rapidly and watching as he covers the dildo in lube. I don't know what possesses me to do it, but I bring my knees up to my chest, staring at the ceiling. He hums in appreciation, and a sharp thrill goes straight to my cock at pleasing him.

"Look at this needy cock slut," he praises, drawing the dildo up and down my crease. "I know this ass can handle this. Just close your eyes and let your body accept it."

With uneven breaths, he teases my rim until the very tip of the dildo breeches me. I suck in a gasp, but it's not one of shock or pain. It's a gasp of pure pleasure. It rips through me as he pushes the dildo further in, and I marvel at how willingly and easily my body accepts it.

"Does it feel good, babe? Do you like this huge dildo up your ass?"

"*Fuck yes...*" I moan, arching my back as he rotates it inside me. "But I want more."

I look up at him as he cocks his pierced brow. He reaches down and strokes his cock in time with his thrusts. "You want my dick?"

"Yes."

"You want me to fuck you?"

"Yes, *please.*"

But my fingers are trembling as they reach for Noah. I want this. I want this so bad, but the nerves are there. It's...it's a completely all-consuming feeling. It's overwhelming, and it makes my jaw chatter in anticipation. Will it hurt? The dildo felt obscenely wonderful, but will his fleshy skin burn in pleasure or pain?

Noah must sense my distress because his eyes soften as he leans up to kiss my cheek. "Are you sure? We can stop this if you want."

I look at those angry hazel eyes and find nothing but tenderness. He would stop if I asked him to, wouldn't he? He would just let this be and walk away without a fight. The thought that he would be willing to do anything to make me comfortable emboldens me. I reach for him, pulling him down so I can mumble against his lips. "I'm ready."

He tortures me with the dildo for another minute before pulling it out. An obscenely wicked slick noise causes my ass to clench in anticipation.

"Condoms?" he asks, setting the dildo down on the nightstand.

I hadn't even thought of that. I don't carry condoms with me during camp. I never had a reason to. I shake my head, but I don't want him to leave. I don't think I'll be satisfied with anything less than him pounding me until I scream. "Are you negative?"

He holds a finger up and reaches down at his discarded pants. He pulls out his phone and scrolls through it. When he's found what he was looking for, he turns it to me, displaying a screenshot of his test results. "For peace of mind."

"I got tested after I caught Jenny cheating on me," I tell him. "I haven't been with anyone since."

"I believe you," he says. He drops his phone and gets on the bed, crawling toward me as I move back until my head hits the headboard. "Are you ready?"

I nod, gripping his shoulders as I wrap my legs around his trim waist. "Yes."

"I'm going to make this so good for you," he promises, running his hands up and down my thighs. "Now, say, 'fuck me, please'."

Panic hits me again. I shouldn't be doing this. I shouldn't be begging Noah to fuck me, but I'm too far gone. There's no stopping this. I *want* this. More than I've ever wanted anything else.

"Fuck me, please," I beg, running my foot up and down his calf, angling myself when he puts his cock against my hole. "Noah, please. Fuck me."

He drops his forehead against mine and pushes. Thanks to the dildo, I swallow him up easily. There's a burn, a slight sting, but the feeling of him bare inside me makes that disappear. I arch my back as his hips meet my ass, holding himself still as I get used to him.

If I liked his fingers and loved the dildo, I have no idea what I feel about this.

Is this what it feels like to be fully whole? Is this what I've denied myself my entire life? Is this exquisite pleasure and pain what's been missing from my lonely existence?

He starts with slow measured thrusts, pausing each time he

bottoms out, holding himself up by his elbows, and staring at me without hesitation. When a crease appears on his brow, I wrinkle my nose in a silent question. It isn't until he brings his thumb up to my eyelids that I realize I'm crying.

He sucks his thumb in his mouth before dragging it down my lips. "I'll take care of you, Jarred. Just let yourself go. I won't let you fall."

I nod as he resumes fucking me. It's sweet and tender for a few minutes but grows into something brutal and animalistic the next. It's like he's losing control, losing the battle with himself to be gentle and patient. There's a light sheen of sweat on his forehead as he grabs my wrists and holds them above my head.

"Open your mouth."

I do, and my eyes roll to the back of my head as he spits in it.

"Swallow."

I do, and his responding moan makes my cock ache. He pulls out and I whine, but quickly it's forgotten when he easily flips my weak body over to get me on all fours. I have to hold onto the headboard as he rams himself back in, spreading my cheeks as he lets a trail of spit run down my ass and into my hole.

"How do you like feeling dirty, babe? Do you like my cock in your ass?" he asks, kneading my ass almost painfully, sure to leave bruises behind. That's fine. Bruise me. Hurt me. Paint me as yours and never let me forget it.

"Yes. Please. Don't stop." If it's possible, I nearly come when he slaps my ass. When he does it again, this time harder, I feel my cock jerk. "Noah...Noah! I think...I think I'm going to come!"

"Do it. Come so I can scoop it all up and fuck it inside you."

The image only sends me over the edge. Before I can come, he quickly flips me over and engulfs my cock in his mouth. The sight of those hazel eyes peering up at me and that lubed-up cock aching makes me explode. I come into his mouth, but he doesn't swallow. He raises my legs in the air, perching them on his shoulders as he spits and lets my cum soak my hole. I scream when he plunges back in, and he's frantic. Frantic enough that every thrust makes my head bang against the headboard.

This new angle is torture, beautiful torture that hits a hidden spot within me. But there's something missing. It's not that *he's* not enough, but *it's* not enough. I can feel a second orgasm building within me, but it's frustratingly out of reach.

"I need more," I whine, holding onto dear life as he reaches down to jack my cock. "Noah! More!"

"I have an idea," he says, out of breath as he pulls out. He leans down and smiles, sultry and seductively as he examines me. "Look how loose that hole is. You want more, babe? You think your virgin ass can take it?"

"Yes, please!"

He reaches for the dildo, and I'm already nodding in anticipation of what's to come. I know what he's going to do, and I ache for it. I crave it. He slathers the dildo with lube and positions it and himself at my entrance. His eyes, glossy and drunk, flick up to me one last time. "You sure?"

I try to push myself against both of them, but he tsks as he pulls away. My lips are set in a tight line as I growl at him. "Fuck me, Noah. Give it to me."

He chuckles darkly and pushes both himself and the toy inside me. I've never felt so full. Never felt so free.

Then it starts fucking vibrating.

I'm fucking shameless. I'm begging him to keep going. I'm twisting and turning and jerking my body. The noises that leave my mouth are foreign to me, and they become part of the brutally lustful and dirty symphony we make.

"Holy shit!" I shout, nearly jumping off the bed at the sensation. "Yes, yes, yes!"

"Fuck! I don't think I can hold it any longer," he groans, his muscles straining with the intensity, his free hand reaching over to jerk my cock. "Give me another one, Jarred. One more."

At his command, I come, and I come *hard*. I paint my chest with proof of what we've done and, with one final brutal stroke, I can feel him filling me up. He's panting and covered in sweat as he collapses on top of me. As he fucks my mouth with his tongue, I can feel him playing with my sore hole, pushing his cum back inside of me.

So dirty. So perfect. So much like everything I've ever wanted but never let myself have.

He flops down on his back beside me and kicks at my leg. "Come here."

I can do nothing but comply with his demand. It takes all my effort to tuck into his side. He rests his arm under my neck as he pulls me to his chest, settling his chin down on the top of my head as he kisses my sweaty forehead. "How do you feel, babe?"

"Good," I answer truthfully, my voice shaky as I melt into him. His hot hard body beneath mine feels like paradise. Once again, I'm shameless. I cling to him for my own sanity. He tenderly strokes between my ass, and I only wince once when he pushes his cum back into my hole.

"Any guilt?"

I swallow harshly. I don't want to think about that. I promised him I wouldn't, but he's the one that brought it up.

So, I answer honestly.

"Yes."

He hums, kissing my temple once again as he murmurs sweet nothings in my ear. "We'll work on that. I have no intentions of letting you go anywhere."

And for one blissful second—away from the guilt and away from the sin—I agree.

I don't want to be anywhere he isn't.

CHAPTER 15
NOAH

As I hold Jarred close to my chest, I can't help but notice how perfect this feels.

I've never been a big cuddler, not with the girls or the guys I've fucked. It seemed like something mandatory to do, so I did, if anything just to let them know I wasn't going to throw them away like trash. But my heart was never in it. I always felt just a little uncomfortable, holding someone close to my chest, letting them hear my heartbeat, but it's different with Jarred.

I want him to hold onto me. I want him to depend on me. I want him to know that I'm here for him. I fucked him hard, probably harder than I should have fucked a virgin, but I don't think he regrets it.

I asked him if he felt any guilt, and I can appreciate his honesty. What's freaking me the fuck out is the cuddling. I love this. I love this almost as much as I loved fucking him. I can feel myself getting attached, but I know better than to cling to someone who can leave me at any second. I know what it's like to crave validation and attention and be denied it—thanks, Mom and Dad.

But I'm letting myself fall into this position because Jarred is special, he has to be. If he wasn't, why would it feel this way?

"What are you thinking about?" I ask him, brushing his sweaty hair off his forehead.

"Jenny," he mumbles against my chest.

My heart stops and my blood heats. "Who the fuck is Jenny?"

He chuckles against my chest. "My ex-wife."

"Care to tell me why the fuck you're thinking about her?"

"She never..." He looks up at me, a vulnerability in those gorgeous brown eyes as he chews on his bottom lip nervously. "I never..."

Understanding dawns on me, and I school my features into something more tender. "You never felt like this with her?"

"No. Our sex life was mediocre at best."

"She cheated on you, didn't she?"

His head snaps up as his jaw drops. "How do you know that?"

"Word gets around," I answer with a shrug, feeling bad because I probably wasn't supposed to know that. "Sorry."

"It's okay," he says, sighing as he kisses my chest. "But yeah, she did. I caught her in the act."

He seems so calm, and I feel angry for him. I've seen how optimistic Jarred is, how kind he is to the campers and counselors, and how hard he works to make sure everything is perfect. He doesn't only have a beautiful body, but a beautiful mind. I can't imagine why anybody wouldn't want him the way I do.

"That must have been rough."

"It was but after I thought about it, I felt almost relieved." He shakes his head and smiles. "She gave me my twins, so I'll always love her for that, but we were just two strangers living together after they'd left home."

"Tell me about your kids," I say, wanting to know more about them, especially since they make his eyes light up the way they are.

"Mary and Parker. They're both twenty-five now."

I resist the urge to make a cheeky comment about the fact that his kids are six years older than I am. "What do they do?"

"Mary teaches third grade in Asheville and just had a baby. Parker is an architect," he says, and I have to smile at the pride in his voice.

"That's cool," I say honestly. "So, you started this camp for them?"

"Yeah. Jenny and I wanted them to grow up with a close bond with God. I wanted to make it a positive experience for them," he says but then something dark passes over his face. Something poisonous and corrupting. "Not everyone is that lucky."

I chew on my lip as my hands twitch for a cigarette. "Can I ask you something?"

"Anything, baby," he says, smiling sweetly at me.

The endearment lights me up. *Baby*. It's such a simple word, but it's everything to me. It's just another little step in the long process of having him realize that what he is and what he wants isn't something to pray away.

It's what furthers my resolve and makes me ask a burning question I have for him. "What we do…why do you think it's so wrong?"

I can feel his harsh gulp against my shoulder. "It's a sin."

"But it's 2023," I argue gently. "Even the Pope is sort of cool with it."

"My father wasn't," he says through gritted teeth, distracting himself by playing with my nipple piercing. "He made that perfectly clear growing up."

Well, that makes sense. Parents can fuck a person up. They can make them think things that aren't true. They can instill beliefs that are plain harmful. My parents taught me that I was worthless without God. His parents probably told him the same thing.

But then why do we have such fundamentally different views about who we are?

"So, it's because of your dad," I say. "I'm going to assume he's long gone now."

He takes a second before speaking again. I don't know when it started, but he's trembling against me. I rub my hands up and down his back as he gathers his courage, the fingers that are playing with my piercing halting in their movements. "When I was thirteen, he caught me kissing a boy. He…"

This makes me sit up, dragging him with me. "What did he do to you?"

"He b-beat me," he says, stuttering through his words, his cheeks going pale.

I can't hide my shock or my outrage as I gasp. "What the fuck! What the fuck was wrong with him!"

"He wanted me to pray away the gay," he confesses, and I see the tears gathering in his eyes. "He thought being gay was something he could beat out of me."

I hate what I'm about to ask, but I need to know. "What would he do?"

"He would...he would make me watch gay porn and beat me if I got hard. He even..."

"Babe," I say, grasping both his cheeks as I press my forehead against his. "He's not here anymore. He can't hurt you."

"He..." He chokes on a sob, wrapping his arms around me as he shudders. "He would make me pray on my knees for hours on end. I would pray until my knees were bruised, and my tongue was dry. I'd pray and pray and pray until he'd just beat me again."

I hold him closer against me, bringing his face to my chest, protecting him from his own memories even though all I want to do is burn the world down at his confession.

That evil fucker. I try not to, but I can picture it. I can picture Jarred —young and perfect—subjected to his father's torturous methods.

It's the awful, soul-crushing, ugly truth. His father tortured him as a child. He took someone innocent and pure and did one of the worst things imaginable. He made Jarred feel like he was a mistake, like his whole existence and who he was had been wrong.

I understand now. I understand why Jarred was so scared to indulge in what is happening between us. I get why it wrecked the living shit out of him. It's not his fault. Maybe it's not even God's fault. It's the fault of his bastard father.

I know I shouldn't think it, but I'm glad his father's dead. I'm glad he's out there rotting somewhere six feet under, unable to hurt Jarred any more than he already has.

I hope Jarred's father suffered in his life. I hope everything he ever loved got taken away from him. I hope he burns in hell for ever daring to do this to his own child.

"You're so strong, babe," I whisper in his ear, fighting back my own tears as I kiss his cheek. "So strong. I can't imagine going through that. You're safe now, okay? You're safe, and you never have to go through that again."

"I'm not strong," he argues, pulling away so his tear-drenched face can look up at me. His lips are quivering, and his eyes are full of so much pain and devastation. "I gave into temptation with you, Noah. I sinned."

"No, your father messed with your head," I say gently, mad at the world but not at him. "He taught you that who you are is wrong and that's bullshit." I pause, brushing his trembling lip with my thumb. "Are you gay, Jarred?"

He sucks in a shuddering breath. Ever so slowly, he nods. He nods and he sobs and there's snot running down his nose and tears kissing his lips. "Yes. I'm...I'm gay."

I don't think he's ever said it aloud before. I'm so fucking proud of him for doing it. Knowing what I know now, I'm so proud that he still came to me. I'm honored that he's shared this with me, and I plan to support him in any way I can.

"How did that feel to say?"

"Scary...but good," he says through a shaky smile, wiping at his nose with the back of his hand. "It felt good."

"I'm here for you. Whatever you need. Just don't push me away," I beg. I'm not used to being vulnerable. I'm not used to opening myself up like this but if it's what Jarred needs, I'll do it. "Please, don't push me away, Jarred."

He snuggles into my chest, hand over my beating heart. "I don't think I can anymore."

Good. He hasn't healed from what happened all those years ago, but I'll help him. I'll be here for him. I'll do whatever it takes to make him realize he's perfect just the way he is.

Because this is turning into more than a fuck, more than a whim, and more than anything I could have ever imagined.

Because I want Jarred. Not just now but maybe always.

CHAPTER 16
NOAH

This is fucking awkward.

As I sit inside the chapel, one part of the big circle that's comprised of campers, I gulp.

It's ministry time, and I have no idea what the fuck I'm doing. The campers are all staring at me expectantly. Patrick and Kendall hang outside of the circle, giving me encouraging looks. I might have let it slip that I was nervous, so they told me they were here for moral support. Honestly, I'm relieved. I know I'm going to fuck this up.

Fuck, I'm only slightly annoyed at Jarred for making me do this.

"So," I say, clapping my hands together when what I really want is a cigarette. "What do we want to talk about today?"

"Aren't you supposed to decide?" Polly asks. She's a sixth grader from South Carolina who's a little too sassy for her own good.

I gulp and chuckle nervously. They're just fucking kids. I can do this. "I guess…I haven't really done this before. I don't talk about God very often."

"Why's that?" Ian asks, pushing his glasses up his nose as he leans forward in his seat.

"Maybe I don't one hundred percent believe in Him?" I answer honestly with a shrug. "Maybe I felt that all my life, He was just shoved down my throat?"

"If you don't believe in God, why are you here?" Michael snaps. He's someone I don't particularly like. I've seen him around camp. He's one of Patrick's campers, and the little brat is always correcting him. He's a bully, and I can say that judging from the way he treats his 'friends'.

I know it's weird to dislike children, but I have an arch-nemesis, and he a twelve-year-old with blue braces.

"That's an excellent question with a long answer."

"I like that you're honest with us," Ian says, smiling gently at me. "Most adults aren't."

Polly raises her hand but speaks before I can say anything. "Maybe we can help you find your faith again."

Okay, this is easy. I can do this. I guess I just have to be honest with them. That's what this whole thing is about, right? Talking about God? "There are just a lot of things I don't agree with."

Chelsea, I think her name is, cocks her head to the side. "Like what?"

"Well, I'm all for abortion. If you're not ready, you're not ready. It's a woman's choice what she does with her body. Fertility treatments are okay. If people want a baby that bad, they deserve one. And…"

I know it's not smart to say, but I'm starting to realize that these kids need to know the truth. I don't want them to think that there aren't those out there who are different. I want them to understand that the world is a big place full of interesting people and, no matter what their differences are, deserve to be treated the same. They deserve to know multiple points of view. Isn't the point of education to teach them how to think for themselves? To give them information and let them decide what *they* want to believe?

"Noah," Kendall interrupts, pulling me out of my own thoughts. She has a worried expression on her face as she looks at Patrick.

"Homosexuality," I say plainly, rubbing my hands up and down my thighs to give them something to do. "I don't believe it's a sin."

"That's disgusting," Michael spits. "A man lying with another man? That's gross!"

"How? How is loving someone gross?" I argue, keeping my voice even and level. I don't want them to think I'm preaching to them. I'm just giving them a different side of an infinite argument, something to consider for themselves. "That's what I don't get. Doesn't God preach about love and acceptance? Does it matter who we choose to be with? Why believe in God if His love is conditional?"

"I don't like where this topic is going," Polly says, looking uncomfortable in her seat. "God teaches us that it's a sin for a man to lie with another man."

"I'm not trying to convince you God isn't real or that he's a dick," I say, trying to appease her. "I'm just speaking what I believe."

"And what you believe is wrong," Michael declares, his fists clenched by his sides. "You're acting as if you're one of them too."

"I am. I like both men and women, and I'm still here," I explain coolly, wondering if they've ever knowingly met a gay person in their lives. "God hasn't smitten me where I stand, has he?"

"Is this where my parents are sending me? Seriously? They would be pissed to hear what you're saying," Michael says, his chair screeching against the wooden floor as he stands.

"Maybe we should cut this group short," Kendall says, rushing into the circle as she holds her hands up in the air. She waves Patrick over with a nervous smile on her face. "Why doesn't everyone take some extra outdoor time? Patrick can lead you all on a hike."

"Oh, okay, yeah," Patrick says, flustered as all the campers look at him. "Um, totally."

My mouth hangs open as they all leave. Great, so much for my first ministry group. I was just trying to be honest with the kids. That's all. I just wanted to teach them something new. I don't think I was forcing my beliefs down their throats, but maybe I was a bit defensive. Maybe I did get a little bit angry.

Why can't they fucking see it? I know they're just kids, but why do they have to have so much hate in their hearts? How is that fair to them? How is that fair to anyone?

"What was that?" Kendall barks once they're all gone, so uncharacteristic of her normally cheerful attitude. "Seriously, Noah?"

"I'm sorry," I spit, taking my beanie off and throwing it on the floor. "I fucked up, alright? I thought I was doing the right thing."

"You can't tell a room full of Catholic children that you're bisexual," she says with her hands planted on her hips. I know she's trying to look menacing, but her pigtails are giving me the opposite effect. "What were you thinking, Noah?"

I hate her tone. I hate how condescending she sounds. I hate that she probably hates gay people too. I fucking hate it.

I hate that parents like Jarred's dad do this to their children. I hate that they make them believe hate is okay. I hate that nobody is doing anything to stop it. I hate the world for just accepting it.

"I'm angry, Kendall. I'm angry that I'm here. I'm angry that their parents and the church are making them believe that being gay is bad," I admit, my voice rising as my anger increases.

"And that's your own opinion," she says calmly. "But these are impressionable children."

"Kendall—"

"I don't mean to say that you're wrong," she rushes out. "The church says it's a sin but…I know gay people."

The way she says it, almost like a hushed secret makes me pause. Still, my retort comes out sarcastic and filled with mocking disbelief. "Really?"

"Yeah," she says with a roll of her eyes. "The people I know that are gay are nice and kind. They're my friends. I don't like thinking that God is going to send them to hell because of who they love."

"Then why aren't you backing me up?" I ask, throwing my hands in the air.

"Because this isn't about you, Noah! It's about Mr. Walker!" she snaps. "He loves this place more than anything and you're threatening to have some of these kids go home because of what you said. There's a way to teach love and forgiveness without doing it the way you did."

Maybe she has a point. I had been thinking of Jarred but not in that way. I had been thinking that I wished there had been someone there for him when he was thirteen, someone to tell him it was okay to be who he is. Maybe I had been thinking that any of these kids could have been Jarred and all they needed to know was that someone accepted them.

I hadn't thought about adult Jarred. I hadn't considered how my words would affect his livelihood. He does love this camp. He made it for his kids, and he prides himself on all that can be accomplished here. Suddenly, I feel like an idiot and a dick.

"I need to warn him, don't I?" I sigh, dropping my head into my hands.

Kendall clicks her tongue and nods. "I think it's for the best."

"Fuck, I really don't want to," I say as I pick up my beanie and stand. Fuck, how am I going to explain this to him?

"I wouldn't either," she says sympathetically. When I'm about halfway through the pews, she stops me. "Oh, and Noah?"

I turn and raise my brows. "Yeah?"

She places her hands over her heart, letting out a happy breath. "I accept and love you for who you are. I just thought you should know that."

I guess I needed to hear that. Here I was, vilifying Kendall when all she was doing was looking out for Jarred. She's the proof right here. The proof that you can be Catholic but still be accepting. She's the proof that maybe, at the end of the day, there's still hope for these kids.

And that thought makes what I'm about to do just a little bit easier.

CHAPTER 17
JARRED

This is amazing.

As I look through the papers scattered around my desk, I feel a sense of pride in my accomplishments. This year, we have doubled the number of campers we normally take in during the summer. Because of that, we'll be able to renovate the counselors' bunks. No, more than that. We'll even be able to upgrade the showers, and the appliances in the common area, maybe even construct another building.

Normally, this would have been something I shared with Jenny, but I find that now all I want to do is tell Noah. I can already picture the look on his face. He'll pretend to not care, but there will be pride in his eyes as he talks to me. He'll kiss me and tell me that it's great. He'll show me those little bits of himself that he keeps locked up. It'll be for me. Just me.

Just like how he was when he fucked me last week. He was a perfect combination of brutal and tender. He opened himself up in the way he took care of me when I told him about my experience growing up. All those disgusting memories came flooding back in but, in his arms, I found that they were easier to deal with.

As if summoned by my own thoughts, Noah walks into my office. He closes the door behind him as he waves, and I stand up to greet him.

"Hey," he murmurs, giving me one of those half-smiles I've come to expect from him.

I, on the other hand, beam at him as I cross my office. Without any prompting, I kiss him. It's just a quick peck on the lips, but it's something I wanted to do. I did it for myself. I did it because I could.

"Hi," I say, feeling a bit sheepish and unsure despite the things we've done. "I was just thinking about you."

"Yeah?" He smirks, running his fingers through my beard. "What about?"

Heat fills my cheeks as I look at the floor. "Well…"

He pinches my chin between his fingers and tips my head up, daring me to meet his dark stare. "Say it, Jarred."

"I was thinking about the other night," I admit, reaching up to run my hands across his broad shoulders. "About how good it felt. About how I want it to happen again."

"Oh, it's going to happen again, babe," he says, thumbing my bottom lip. Something flashes through his face as he drops his hand and sighs. "Well, maybe not after I tell you what I have to say."

I furrow my brows as I chase the feeling of his hands on me. "What is it?"

"I fucked up."

"What did you do?"

"I was in ministry, and I may or may not have outed myself…" He bites at his bottom lip as he stares at me hesitantly. He takes a single step back and runs a hand down his mouth. "I might have also told the kids I don't believe in God…"

I jerk my head. "You what?"

"I'm sorry," he says, rushing up to grab my hands and help me sit on the edge of my desk. "They were just asking all these questions, and I didn't want to lie to them. I…honestly, I have no idea what the fuck happened."

Dazed, I ask. "How did they react?"

"Some were quiet, others were grossed out, but—um—one threatened to call his parents."

"Oh," I rasp, my stomach filling with a sense of unease as I try to come to terms with his words. Although Noah's never hidden who he is, I never thought he'd actually tell the kids he's bisexual. I mean, it's not exactly a topic I'd want my campers to address during a casual youth ministry. Before I can say anything, Noah speaks.

"I'm sorry. I'm so sorry," he says, looking uncharacteristically worried. "Kendall made me see that it wasn't about me. I don't want to ruin what you've built. I kind of like it here."

"I..." I settle my thoughts, reaching inside of me to try and decipher what exactly it is I'm feeling. Surprisingly, I find the obvious one missing. "I'm not angry."

His pierced brow shoots up to his hairline. "You're not?"

"No," I say truthfully, reaching to grab his wrists and pull him between my spread thighs. "Lying is a sin and you spoke your truth. It's okay to have doubts, and the kids need to know this. Sometimes we stray, but the Lord will always be there for us."

He scoffs. "Yeah, we'll revisit that topic later."

I swallow harshly. "You really don't believe in God?"

"Why would I?" he says, his tone angry, and I can feel the tension in his body through his wrists. "He was crammed down my throat my entire life. I'm repulsed by the idea of God."

From all I know about Noah, I should have seen that coming. He wasn't exactly enthused about coming to this particular camp. During mass, he doesn't bow his head and pray with us. He doesn't even take communion. But there's something about hearing this confirmation that unsettles me.

What could a life without God be like? I guess I never really thought that was an option. As soon as I was born, I was baptized. I grew up going to Sunday school and was even an altar boy. God has always been there in the back of every decision and every act. He's so deeply ingrained within me that I can't imagine ever being without Him.

"Why are you repulsed by Him?" I ask, feeling sick even saying those words.

The tips of his ears turn red as he grinds his teeth. Behind the angry façade, I can see that he's the slightest bit embarrassed by his following words. "My parents...they love God more than they love me."

My heart softens for him. "Noah..."

"It's true," he rushes out. "I was always in second place with them. God before everything. God before anything. God before your own fucking son."

"Is that why they sent you here?"

"Yeah. I wasn't living the way God would want me to and it pissed them off. Apparently enough for them to hold my college fund hostage," he snarks with a roll of his eyes, although I can see the brief flash of pain in his eyes. "I'm not worth their unconditional love, not if God's involved."

"Noah," I say, licking my lips as I run my hands up his arms soothingly. "That's not true."

I think about my own kids—though I try to ignore the reminder that Noah's younger than they are—and I can never imagine loving anything more than them. I know that I'm supposed to love God first. That's the whole point of a myriad of gospels. God is before everything but that's just not true for me. There's nothing I wouldn't do for my twins, nothing I wouldn't sacrifice for them.

And if they ever 'lived the way God didn't want them to', I don't think I'd force them to come to a place they hate. I certainly wouldn't risk their future and their education to prove a point.

"Sometimes I wonder if they even love me at all."

"Baby. Come here," I say sternly. I'm not usually the one to take this tone in our dynamic, but I need him to stop saying such miserable things. He takes a slow step forward and drops his head against the crook of my neck, his soft exhale tickling my skin. I rub my hands up and down his back while I nuzzle the side of his head, briefly kissing his ear. "You are absolutely incredible. You're funny in a really crude type of way. You showed how loyal you are when you stood up for Patrick. You cared about me when I told you about my past. What's not to love about you?"

"I wish my parents could feel that way about me," he confesses, trembling in my arms. "I wish I was worthy of that love."

"You are worthy of it," I whisper, kissing his ear once again "Who could be foolish enough not to love you?"

"I wish I could believe that," he chuckles.

I grip him tighter. I don't like the way he's thinking. Noah, despite his flaws, is perfect. Despite his anger, his crudeness, his feigned indifference, is absolutely magnificent. He's one of a kind. He managed to break through my shell and make me realize I have the freedom to act on my wants, no matter how wrong they are. He was able to give me something I never believed I could have. He did this all with courage in his heart and hidden compassion brimming under the surface.

An idea comes to me. It's one that I would normally try to push away, but Noah makes me want to explore all those parts of me I've kept hidden. "Let me show you how special you are."

He looks confused when he pulls away, but his eyes darken as I play with the edge of his T-shirt, pushing it up to expose the thin trail of hair that leads down his stomach and disappears beneath his pants. His confidence is regained when he steps back to rip off his shirt in anticipation of what he can sense is coming. I love that he's back to what I know, self-assured and positively daunting.

I lean forward into temptation and lick at his nipple, my eyes closing and my voice moaning as I wrap my tongue around the little barbell pierced there. I give him wet kisses, sucking the piercing into my mouth hungrily. I kiss it before speaking and looking up at him. "I love these. The first time I saw them, I just wanted to suck on them until I left a bruise."

"Do it," he commands, strong hands palming the back of my head as he yanks me against his chest. "Claim me."

And I do. My enthusiasm is boundless as I lap at his other nipple, tonguing the barbell and lightly yanking on it with my teeth. He lets out a deep groan that shoots straight to my cock when I let my hand play with his other piercing. But it's not enough. I've gotten a hint of the taste of his skin, just a peak at the salty tang of his body, and I want more.

I'm greedy and gluttonous as I push him back and drop to my knees. It aches a bit, but I mask my wince as my fingers immediately fly to his belt. I don't even know what I'm doing. I've never sucked a man off before, although I imagined it late in the night when my inhibitions were low, and my dreams ran amuck.

"You're going to suck me?" he asks, his voice deep and husky as I pull down his pants and underwear, just over his ass, trapping his legs in place. I let out an unrecognizable high-pitched whine when he smacks me in the face with his cock.

It's a thing of beauty. It's long and hard, thick in all the right places. It's slightly larger than mine, just in girth, and I know I'm going to have a rough time wrapping my lips around it. But I want the challenge. I want to ache as I take him in. I want to be stuffed so full of him I could choke on his cock happily.

"Give it to me," I beg, whining yet again when he pulls his cock away just as my lips get close enough to smell his musk. "*Noah.*"

He chuckles darkly as he pushes his clothes all the way down, standing gloriously naked in front of me, all of that youth and beauty on display just for me. "You want it so bad, don't you babe?"

I nod rapidly as he lifts his cock, giving me a peak of the piercing nestled on the underside just at the base. "Please, Noah."

"Open up," he whispers huskily, prying my jaw open with his thumb, making sure to rub it on my tongue for a brief second. "Let me feed you my dick."

I open up as he demands, and he slowly slides the tip of his cock into my mouth. I want to take more. I want to take all of it, but he's controlling the pace and in charge of the amount I'm given. It's torture to have my mouth open like this—hungry and waiting—but be denied what I want more than anything else. He gets himself halfway in my mouth and holds it there, threading one hand through my hair as he looks down at me fondly. Finally, and with excruciating care, he gives me every single inch of him.

He's thick and throbbing in my mouth, so utterly male that it makes my cock jerk with a hit of precum that dampens my underwear. The fabric is sticky as he continues to fuck my face slowly, but I don't dare touch myself.

Not yet. Not until he says I can.

He rests both hands on either side of my face and when I give him one deep suck, hollowing my cheeks and lightly scraping my teeth against his sensitive skin, he groans. "Jarred...*babe*...get me in there. Suck me deeper."

I do as he demands. He's letting me take control now, and I'm not going to disappoint. I bob my head up and down his cock, not at all ashamed or embarrassed by how eager I am to make him come. I want to worship him, but my patience is thin. I want to taste that salty cum in my mouth. I want that pleasure-stricken expression on his face. I want to be the only one who makes him feel this fucking *good.*

I take him all the way to the back of my throat and—with a deep breath and a shit ton of confidence I don't have—I let him in until I'm deepthroating his cock. I can feel the drool spilling out of my mouth and onto the floor. I can feel the prickling of tears in my eyes, but I don't dare back off. Not when his eyes widen in surprise and those gloriously lithe thighs tighten by how hard he's trying not to shove himself in any further.

"So pretty. Look at those tears," he hums, skating his thumb over my cheek to pad at the wetness. He brings it to his lips and sucks it into his mouth. Something flashes in those dark eyes, and he smirks as he parts his legs and reaches behind him. "Get your fingers in my ass."

I pull off him quickly. Did he just say what I think he said? I've never been anywhere near his ass. I just always assumed that he liked to be on top, that he didn't want anyone going anywhere near his hole, but he just told me to go there. For a brief moment, I feel so stupid. Here he is, wantonly and confidently demanding I fuck him, so in charge and secure of his own masculinity.

I will admit that when he fucked me—when I felt him deep inside me—I couldn't ignore the feeling of being less than a man. I loved every second of it, don't get me wrong, but that nagging itch in my mind wouldn't go away. Now, I feel like an idiot for ever thinking that. If Noah—mysterious, angry, so fucking perfect Noah—can ask me to fuck him then there's nothing to be ashamed of.

My fingers are trembling as I suck them into my mouth, making sure to get them nice and wet before I reach around him. I bump his hands on the way and notice that he's holding his spread cheeks apart for me. I blindly move my finger around until I feel his puckered hole, and I almost want to ask him to turn around so I can get a nice long look at it. I bet it's perfect, pink, so eager to swallow me up.

"Fuck me," he says quietly, guiding my finger until it's pressing into him. He throws his head back with a low moan as he guides me in, simultaneously pressing his cock against my lips. "Suck me off and finger fuck me until I come."

When he says it like that—so dirty and sinful—I can't refuse. I slowly start to thrust into him with my finger while I suck his cock back into my mouth. I get the burst of taste on my tongue that tells me how much he's loving this. His hands are still holding apart his cheeks, and his legs are wobbly as I hollow out my cheeks.

"Jarred...*f-fuck*...this won't last much longer," he breathes, letting his cheeks go so he can hunch over and grip my shoulders. "Keep fucking me like that and...and..."

But he doesn't get to finish his sentence as he explodes in my mouth. I catch all of his cum on my tongue, and my own cock is happy and satisfied with how *incredible* it tastes.

Just as I'm about to swallow, he stops me with a hand on my jaw, looking deceptively angry and carnal as he shakes his head. "Don't swallow. Show it to me."

My cheeks tinge pink as I open my mouth, his cum pooling on my tongue, some of it dripping down onto the floor with just how much there is.

"Mmm," he moans, stroking my cheek as he gulps audibly. "Use it to jack yourself off. *Don't* swallow."

I awkwardly hold his cum in my mouth as I hastily rip my pants open. I don't even have time to fumble them down my thighs because I'm so desperate to get off. Having him in my mouth has put me just on the edge of my sanity, wound so tight I know it'll only take a few tugs before I spill my release.

"Spit," he commands, smiling prettily when I do as he says and let his cum coat my length. "Stroke your cock."

As predicted, it only takes a second. That's it. Just one long stroke, one heavy-handed thrust into my fist, and I'm spilling all over. It hits my black shirt and trickles down onto my pants, creating an obscene stain I know I'll have to cover up before I leave my office.

"How..." I swallow harshly, feeling a pleasurable burn in my throat as I croak out my words. "How did I do?"

His face softens as he falls to his knees in front of me. He bends down to lick a stripe up my shaft that makes me shudder. He presses kisses to my fabric-covered chest until he nestles his nose at the crook of my neck. After breathing me in, his lips press against mine in a sweet embrace so different from his earlier tone. "Fuck, you were perfect. Did you like my cock in your mouth?"

"Yes," I whisper, knowing that my thoughts and my wants—no matter how wrong they are—are safe with him.

"Good," he coos, petting my hair as he nibbles at my lower lip. "Because, babe, we're so doing that again."

And I smile because that sounds perfectly good to me.

CHAPTER 18
NOAH

My breaths are heavy and ragged, my pulse pounding in the side of my neck, sweat beading my hairline as I savagely move my hand up and down mine and Jarred's joined cocks. *Fuck*, he feels so good.

It's been two weeks of this. Two weeks of sneaking away to spend blissful time together getting each other off. Today was no different, the only thing that changed was that Jarred and I couldn't control ourselves and wait for the cover of darkness. It's his fault, really. How did he expect me to react when he sucked on that lunchtime popsicle like he was imagining it was my cock?

It took all my self-control to not shove him onto his knees in the middle of the dining hall. I somehow managed to get him to the van parked in the back of the camp without anyone seeing us and the second we were alone, shoved my cock into that beautiful mouth.

"W—what did you call this?" he asks breathlessly, back arching the floor, his limbs having enough room to stretch out in ecstasy since we're hiding out in the seatless back of the van.

"Frotting," I choke out, spitting once again on our cocks to slick up my movements. "You like?"

"I love...harder...*Noah*." He raises his hands to grip the back of my neck, dragging me down to him to flick his tongue against the metal of my lip piercing. "I'm going to..."

He bursts in my hands, sticky wet ropes of cum coating my fingers. I follow right after him, grunting and groaning as I paint his bare chest with my cum. "You're so fucking hot when you come."

"That was amazing," he chuckles breathlessly, reaching for a discarded rag in the corner to clean us up. "Can we do that again?"

I smile down sweetly at him. He looks so flushed, beautifully excited, and deliriously happy, and I did that. He's been getting better about asking for what he wants, sexually and otherwise. He's started to embrace the time we've spent together—vocal and enthusiastic—and always begging for more.

"Fuck yeah we can, but not right now," I tease, trailing my finger up his spent cock which twitches at the sensitivity. "Both of our dicks need a break."

He pouts but nods, absentmindedly as he traces my eyebrow piercing, amusing himself with fiddling with the little barbell at the end of it. "Right. We should probably get back before anybody notices we're gone."

"Nobody is going to notice." I bite the corner of my lip as an idea comes to me. I laugh and bring his fingers to my lips, teasingly biting them. "Let's skip."

"Skip? What are we? In high school?" He snorts but then blanches, already sensing my incoming joke. "Don't answer that."

I roll my eyes as I drape myself over him, bracketing his head with my arms as I start pressing feather-light kisses on his face. "I'm scheduled for van duty right now, and I don't have a studio session until later today. You can get Father Matteo and Kendall to watch over the camp. Let's go somewhere. Just you and me."

I know I haven't voiced it, but I think that all this sneaking around has been getting to me. I crave what I have with Jarred, always wanting his body, always yearning for his thoughts, always giving him parts of me I've never given anybody else, but there's a limit to that. I've been slowly feeling it as the weeks have gone by. It's not enough to stop whatever it is we're doing, but it is enough for me to want just a little escape. To want to go somewhere where we don't have to hide. Where he can see how good this could feel out in the open.

"Where would we go?" Jarred worries his bottom lip. I can tell that he's thinking this over way too much. I mean, I get why he wouldn't want to be seen out in public with me, but I've thought this through enough for the both of us. It's about a two-hour drive from here, in the middle of nowhere, where nobody can recognize us. He should know by now I'd never put him at risk.

"Well, I saw a sign three towns over for mini golf."

"Mini golf?" he chuckles. "I haven't played that in twenty years."

"See? It'll be fun," I say, poking at his side. "You haven't played it since before I was born."

Once again, he pouts adorably, the tips of his ears burning red. "Please, don't put it that way."

"So, what do you say?"

He takes a deep breath and smiles sheepishly. "Okay?"

I'll take it.

"Perfect," I say, slapping his hip as I toss him his shirt. "You go tell Father Matteo you're leaving, and I'll get the van ready."

He nods and leaves with a parting kiss. It doesn't take him long to tell them we're leaving before he's already back in the van. We drive in companionable silence, listening quietly to music, our hands intertwined between our seats. Once we get there, I follow the signs for the mini golf place I noticed last time I came to this town to pick up some supplies. Nobody bats an eye as we approach the little kiosk, pay, and get our clubs.

It becomes increasingly apparent ten minutes in that I have no idea how to fucking play mini golf, but Jarred just laughs it off, perfectly doing...whatever it is you do in mini golf.

"I told you this would be fun," I say, smiling when he does this adorable little clap when he sinks the ball into the hole. "So, twenty years since the last time you played? It doesn't look like it."

"Yeah. Jenny and I took the kids when they were five. They loved it," he says but something pinches at his expression as we move on to the next lane. "Now that I think about it, it might have been the last time we actually had fun together as a family."

"Not the greatest relationship," I blurt sarcastically then I curse. "Shit, I'm overstepping."

He smiles at me with a soft shake of his head, laughing a little under his breath as I set up for my turn. "No, you're not. Jenny and I got married right out of high school. It was one of those comfortable kinds of love. Safe, I think."

"I can't imagine you in high school," I snort. "Let me guess. You wore a lot of flannel."

"No, I was actually the captain of the football and basketball team," he says with a roll of his eyes and a proud smirk on his lips. "I played a little of both in college too."

"What's your degree in?" I ask. I poke my tongue out as I try to focus on the ball in front of me, but I miss it by way more than a few inches and frown. I sigh in exasperation and turn back to him. "Damn."

"Catholic Theology."

"Wow. That sounds…"

Boring. It sounds fucking boring as hell.

Jarred sobers, holding the bright pink ball in his hand for two seconds too long before setting it down, not making eye contact with me as he speaks. "It was what my dad wanted."

Right. That piece of shit. I swear if I could resurrect him just to kill him myself I would. I hate the fact that I've even remotely managed to steer the conversation in that direction. So, I change the subject. "Well, I was artsy, which you can probably guess."

"A tortured artist," he says teasingly with a sly smirk. "Lots of metal music and grungy outfits."

"Nah, I was…" I struggle for the word that can aptly describe my circumstances growing up. "Perfect. The perfect kid who got perfect grades and acted perfectly at church."

He frowns, stilling and ignoring the fact that it's his turn and people are sure to catch up with us. "That doesn't seem like you. Not that you're not perfect. That's not what I meant—"

"I know what you meant. I just acted exactly like my parents wanted me to. I did everything they asked for. It wasn't until I left for college that I realized how trapped I was."

It was a life of suppressing who I really was. It was constant quips about the state of my hair and the weight of the scale. It was always being told to be quiet, be invisible, be forgettable. It was being consistently told that my mere existence was an inconvenience and the least I could do was make myself as small as possible to make up for that.

"Is that why you're so angry sometimes? Like when you first got here?"

I suck in a sharp breath at his question. I'm not...well...maybe I am a little angry. Maybe it does have something to do with the fact that my parents—perfect pious members of our privileged society—only had me because they needed to. I won't lie. I grew up with everything I could ever want but there were strings. Strings tied to my limbs that they pulled like effortless puppeteers.

"I guess anger came naturally," I say calmly, already feeling the stirrings of rage bubbling when I think of my parents. The bitter resentment of my strict upbringing boiling inside me. But then I look at Jarred. Patient, sweet, timid Jarred and I smile. "I'm not angry anymore, though."

His lips twitch as he scoots closer to me, shyly blushing as he bites his bottom lip. "No?"

"No," I whisper back softly, and then because I can't help it— "Not when I have such a wise presence to guide me."

He glares at me. "The jokes are getting old."

"Like you."

"Shithead," he laughs, shoving at my arm playfully. I bask in his unfiltered joy, and I can't control myself as I link my hand with his.

"You cursed. I didn't think you had it in you."

"I curse plenty." He rolls his eyes dramatically as he squeezes my fingers. He doesn't even look around. He doesn't even care, and it just makes me even happier.

So, I take a risk. I lean into him, my lips brushing lightly against his ear. "Yeah, when I make you come you do."

Jarred chuckles and that beautiful blush coats his tan cheeks. He turns his head slightly, our lips mere inches away. His eyes flicker from mine to my lips but then something changes. His eyes widen and he yanks himself away from me, fumbling with his club, and dropping it on the ground. I cock my head to the side at his sudden change and then glance behind me where his eyes are locked.

I feel like punching something when I see a younger couple with their kids, their faces pinched in disgust as they usher their children away from us. Fuckers. Can't mind their own fucking business.

"Hey," I say to Jarred, placing a hand on his heated cheek. "Don't let them bother you."

He pulls away from me quickly, picking up his club. He doesn't look at me as he fiddles with it in his hands. "Can we go? I think we've left the camp alone long enough."

I hate this. I hate that the amazing day we were having is ruined. I hate that the progress we've made has been recessed again. All because of a couple of homophobes that don't matter at all.

I recognize the look on Jarred's face. Fear. Shame. Guilt. All those ugly emotions that we had been slowly moving past. All crumbled and destroyed.

But I don't push him. I can't push him. He's wormed his way inside of me, made a home in all the dark spots, and made me more patient.

"Yeah, babe. We can go."

CHAPTER 19
JARRED

The next two weeks pass by in a blur of sex and sweat and sweetness.

After that disastrous time at the mini-golf course, Noah made sure to comfort me. Although the lingering feeling of guilt and shame still bubbles in my stomach at the thought of those parents' faces, Noah takes it all away with his sweet touches and gentle tone.

Noah and I can't seem to keep our hands off each other. Every spare minute, we're trading secrets and promises in the dark. Every day, I promise myself that next time will be the last time, the only time, but I break that every time his lips hit mine.

There's something scandalizing about sitting in the church pews this Sunday, my ass sore and tender as I try to pay attention to today's gospel. I'm usually really good at keeping myself checked into the Holy Words, but I can't stop looking at Noah. He's holding his Bible up to his face—more than likely not even reading it—but his eyes are looking at me through those thick dark lashes.

All I can see when I look at him is the moment we shared yesterday afternoon. Noah had been on van duty, and I made an excuse to go into town so I could spend some time with him. He told me about what he does at UNC, his friends, and even his pet dog that his friend is watching over the summer. I told him about the time I broke my arm when I was eight because I wasn't paying attention to the sidewalk in front of me and hit a rock. He surprised me with his ability to sing along to top hits from the sixties. He laughed and cringed when I showed him I was double-jointed.

Those little moments, these tiny tidbits all make him so much more endearing. He's not just a body that I've been losing myself in, ignoring all the obvious reasons why I shouldn't. He's a real person—kind, funny, sarcastic, loyal—and I'm starting to like all those little pieces of him.

Oh, and I also can't forget the way he forced my legs up to my shoulders and fucked me on the hood of the van in a forest road. Hence my very sore and very happy ass.

I tear my gaze away from him just as the camper reading the gospel finishes and recites the parting lines.

"Praise to you Lord Jesus Christ," I say, bowing my head as we all take a seat. I manage to find a way to not sneak another look at Noah and focus instead on Father Matteo.

"Brothers and sisters, how is everyone feeling?" Father Matteo asks, charming as he smiles at all of us. There are excited murmurs that get whispered back to him and his smile only widens. "That's wonderful. I'd like for us to reflect on this week's gospel. God asked Abraham to take his only son up to the mountain. Who was paying attention?" Sadly, I was not, but that gets made up for when a dozen hands shoot up in the air. "Good. What did God ask of Abraham after that?"

Kendall beams when Father Matteo points at her. She sits up straight and proud as she answers. "God asked Abraham to kill his son, Isaac."

"And why do we think he did that?"

"He wanted to test Abraham's loyalty to him," Bryce says, calling out the answer before Father Matteo even picks him. I try not to let myself prickle with irritation.

"And why would he need to do that?" Father Matteo asks, ripping me away from my stewing. When no one raises their hands, he smirks. "I see. This is where this gospel becomes a bit controversial. If God is loving, why would he ask Abraham to kill his only son? The gospel says that God didn't let Abraham kill Isaac because he wanted to test his obedience."

I nod along with his words. God does ask us for obedience. In return for everything He gives us, all He wants in return is our undying devotion. When you take a step back and look at it, it doesn't seem all too unreasonable. He gave us life, He gave us free will, and all He asks is that we do what He says. Doesn't that seem easy to give in comparison to all we have?

But my stomach drops. I haven't been obedient. I haven't been following what He would want. I try not to let that reminder sour my mood. No, it's just...Noah and I...but I can't seem to make heads or tails of my thoughts.

"I think God wanted to see how much Abraham would sacrifice for Him," Father Matteo continues, coming down to the center of the pews as he delivers his homily. "Sacrifice is something I want to discuss today. How much would we give up for God?"

I gulp audibly and wonder if everyone can see how I'm starting to sweat. Sacrifice isn't meant to be easy. Sacrifice is meant to be challenging, it's meant to push us, to show our true loyalty, and to test our resolve. Sacrifice involves giving up the things you want because you know it's for the best.

But I've been selfish. Noah...*we've* been selfish. Suddenly, I don't look at our moment yesterday with excitable joy. It's no longer tender and sweet. It's dirty—but not in a good way—and sinful. I look back at him and see that he's as aloof as ever. Is this not affecting him? Is he not freaking out the way I am? How is he so okay with what we're doing?

But I see the twitch in his jaw, the slight show of interest in his dark eyes, and I desperately want to know what he's thinking.

"Isn't that the point of love? Giving up something for the benefit of others? Doing the right thing, even though we know how difficult it is?" Father Matteo asks, his eyes zeroing in on me and my guilt only increasing. He stares at me for a beat. Can he see it written all over my face? Can he see...*sinner* painted across my forehead? Can he sense that I've forsaken everything I was raised to believe?

He smiles softly before turning back to the congregation. "Reflect on that. Think to yourself, what would you give up for love?"

I love God. I love that He's blessed me with my twins and given me a comfortable life. When my father was beating me for my sins and forcing me to pray away my sins, all I could cling to was the fact that God would save me. That God would stop the torture I was experiencing, and He did. I never thought that God was to blame for what I went through. God cared for me and saw me through it. Because of that, I devoted my life to Him. I love Him with every ounce of my being.

I don't love Noah. I know that for certain. I like Noah…a lot. I'm starting to care for him in a way I never thought possible, but it's not love. Romantic love between him and I…that would cross a line, wouldn't it? God could never forgive that. Man shall not lie with another man and marriage and love are meant for man and woman. That leads to the question that Father Matteo asked us today.

What would we sacrifice for God?

"I believe in the Holy Spirit, the holy catholic church, the communion of the saints, the forgiveness of sins, and the resurrection of the body…"

I mumble along because I know every part of mass by heart, but my mind is somewhere else. It's in a state of extreme turmoil, brewing with all the dangerous thoughts I've tried to keep buried. When it's just Noah and I, it's so easy to forget about God. He literally fucks God right out of me. But here, in His holy church, it all comes slamming right back.

Mass progresses as usual, and I go about the motions in a monotonous blur. I can sense that Noah glances at me every now and then—I can sense his smoldering stare as if it's my own—but I can't look back. God is watching. God is judging. God is vengeful, and I want so deeply to be forgiven.

Once the mass has ended, I hastily jump out of my seat. I don't think Noah would approach me here—we always try to keep ourselves separate in public—but I can't risk it. I practically barrel through the campers and counselors, trying to run away from my guilt. I'm not lucky, however, because Father Matteo spots me and stops me just as I'm leaving the church.

"Jarred," he says, halting me with a gentle hand on my elbow. "Did you like today's homily?"

"It was…" I gulp, trying to scramble for words that will hide my obvious distress. "It was very enlightening, Father."

He furrows his brows at my choice of words but quickly schools his face into something more passive and accepting. "What did you think of it?"

"I think you're right. I think that we have to give up the things we love for God." I bluster, glancing nervously around at the campers who are ignoring this conversation. Or maybe they're not. Maybe they can sense the sinner in the Holy Place. They can zero in on—

"Jarred…no," Father Matteo says, shaking his head as he frowns. "That wasn't the point—"

"It was an amazing mass, Father," I rush out, giving him a curt nod and a weak smile. "I look forward to next Sunday."

"Jarred, wait—"

But I'm already walking away from him with one destination in mind. I know that I was trying to avoid Noah earlier, but I've changed my mind. I need to be strong. I need to have courage. I need to do the hard thing and sacrifice what I want and what I love.

I don't love Noah—I can't—but…

The way he smiles down at me when I'm on my knees, looking at me like I'm something precious to take care of. The way his fingers walk down my spine and rest gently on my hole after he's fucked me. The way he curls me into his firm chest, whispering promises and secrets and reassurances and vows deep into the dusk to try and comfort me.

This needs to end. For good. There's no more I can give him. There's no more I can deny God. There's no more I can sin before I'm bound to hell for my disobedience and treachery.

I head to the art studio because I know him that well. He likes to draw. He's sketched me before—just my face—but I marveled at all the intricate details he managed to capture. Sometimes he'll come to my cabin after being at the studio and those paint-covered hands will glide down my body in wicked ways. He's so talented too. You can almost feel his love and his passion for what he creates. He's a visionary. He—

Sacrifice. The things we sacrifice for God.

I enter the art studio, making sure to check over my shoulder to ensure that nobody's watching. When the coast is clear, I slink in and find Noah exactly where I thought he would be. It's hot outside, and the studio doesn't have air conditioning, so he's gloriously shirtless as he paints. His teeth are playing with his lip piercing, pulling and twisting it in concentration as his brush strokes the canvas.

Something in him that calls to me must call to him because he turns as if he can sense I'm here without seeing me. He smirks—beautiful and tinged with mischief—as he sets his brush down. "Hey, handsome."

"What are you drawing?" I ask absentmindedly, stepping up and reaching for his canvas, but I pull back because I'm afraid of ruining it.

"You're telling me you can't make it out?" he chuckles, intertwining his fingers with mine as he pulls me closer. "It's you."

And now that he's said it, I can see it. It's me—naked—spread out on a cloud of white, grey, and dark yellow streaks. He's managed to capture every inch of my body perfectly, so subtle too, and lifelike. I almost glow right off the page, and my breath is taken away.

Is this how he sees me? Almost like a work of art? Perfect lines and angles and softness that I can't see in myself?

"It's...amazing," I gasp softly, unable to hide my smile. "Noah..."

"Well, I had an amazing inspiration. Don't worry, no one's going to see it. I keep all my paintings locked up when I leave," he assures me. He winds his arms around my waist from behind and kisses the back of my neck. "Fuck, how is it that I miss you already?"

I'm so lost in the beauty that is in front of me that I barely have time to react as Noah reaches for my chin and tips my head back so he can brush his lips against mine. I shudder but remember myself. I came in here for a reason.

I rip my lips away. "We can't."

"What..." he backs up and spins me on my heels. "Why?"

"You heard Father Matteo's homily," I croak, swallowing dryly. "Sometimes, we need to sacrifice things for God."

"No," he murmurs, cocking his head to the side as he frowns. "That's not what I heard."

"It's what he meant," I say adamantly and, because I know I can't control myself around him, I give him some space. "I can't do this with you anymore."

And then the curtain drops. All of Noah's exquisite vulnerability and openness fade quickly. In its place is nothing but that repressed anger and apathy. His jaw is clenched tight as he nods. "Fine."

I raise my brows in shock. "Fine?"

"Fuck. What do you want me to say, Jarred? I...I told you things about me," he says, fists clenching and unclenching angrily at his sides. "I'm tired of feeling like I'm not worth anything. I...I need to know my worth."

He did say that. I feel like shit. Noah did confide in me. He told me about the way his parents treat him, and the disinterest they have in him. He opened up to me and showed me his biggest insecurity, and I've just thrown it back in his face.

"Noah, baby, it's not about that," I plead, reaching for his hand. "It's not about you—"

He yanks his hand away harshly. "I was very clear with you. You had to be all in or nothing could come of this."

"Noah, I'm sorry," I whisper feeling tears in my heart start to form, the pain of sacrifice looming high above me, the consequences of my sins rearing their ugly heads.

"You shouldn't be. I feel sorry for you," he states, more calmly this time and with a hint of pitying remorse. "I'm sorry you have to hide. I'm sorry that you can't give yourself what you want. I'm sorry that you seem to hate yourself."

I suck in a sharp breath. "That's...that's not fair."

"Isn't it?" he questions, shaking his head in exasperation. He rips off his beanie and runs his hand through his hair, frustration bleeding through his familiar action. "What your dad did to you was hell. I don't expect you to magically forget what happened to you, but I wish that I could make you see how right this is between us. I can't. Only you can do that."

"I..." I'm at a loss for words. I don't want his pity. I don't want his remorse. I don't want his unfiltered analysis of my own mind. "You don't get it."

"Maybe I don't," he says with a soft shrug. He fiddles with the beanie in his hands, uncharacteristically vulnerable with weak eyes that won't meet mine. "I like being with you but not like this. I don't think I deserve to be your sin."

I swallow harshly. I don't like him like this. I don't want him to think there's anything wrong with him, even though God knows there is. Our depravity will bite us in the ass, but I want to wipe that look off his face. So, I gather more courage. I leave God in the background, something that comes so easily when I'm with Noah. "When I'm with you, I can forget all of that. I can let myself enjoy what we do together."

"But…?"

I spill the ugly truth. "But it'll send me to hell."

He sighs dramatically, closing his eyes as he scowls. "I hate that you still believe that."

"Noah—"

"I'm feeling things for you. I actually fucking like you," he confesses, meeting my gaze, his dark eyes no longer angry. "I like you as more than a fuck. I like you a lot. *You*."

"I feel the same way," I admit, something warm unfurling in my chest.

Noah makes me feel…happy. Have I ever actually felt that before? I'm happy in my relationship with God, in His love, but has it ever been like this? Did my heart ever skip a beat at the mention of His name? Does a simple whisper of a memory of Him cause an uninhibited thrill to shoot through me? Did I want to do anything—*everything*—just to make Him smile with pride?

"I feel the same way," I say, inching toward Noah almost involuntarily. I cup his angular face in my hands, brushing my thumb against the scruff on his cheek, enjoying every inch of *man* under my fingertips. "I like you, Noah."

"I'm not going to beg for you," he whispers, resting his forehead against mine. "No matter how much I want to."

"I don't want you to. I want…"

"What do you want?" he asks, flashing his eyes up to mine. He licks his lips slowly, and I track that movement like a dying man tracks the light of God. "Babe…"

I lean forward and brush my lips against his, ghosting my breath over his mouth, breathing him in. "You."

And then it all happens so quickly. Without any finesses and without any grace, I slam my lips down on his. I'm so hungry for him, so perfectly weak to my knees to be with him. God. God is flashing through my mind. God is judging me. God is berating me. God will hate me.

But Noah's lips take it all away.

Before I know what I'm doing, I'm yanking his pants down to his ankles and falling to my knees. I'll worship him. I'll make him my god for however long this lasts. Because I'm a weak man. I'm a fractured soul. I'm forsaken and lost in Noah's glory.

I take him into my mouth with a loud groan, wrapping my lips around his cock and forcing him down my throat. It's messy and sloppy and I'm sure he's had better, but it's just a testament to how much I want him right now.

"P-Please…" I beg, rutting myself against his leg as I press kisses all over his cock. "Please, fuck me."

He yanks me up to my legs and whirls me around. He quickly slams me down on the nearest table, ignoring the fact that paint is splattering all over us. He drags my pants and underwear down and leaves them around the top of my thighs, his arm braced against my back, effectively pinning me in place.

"Look at this ass," he mumbles, and there's a slick wet sensation across my cheeks. I look back and see that he's dipped his fingers in paint and there are now prominent handprints on my ass. "I want you to be mine, Jarred. I want it so bad."

"Me too," I admit brokenly, savagely banging my head against the table in frustration. "Make me yours, baby."

"I don't have anything on me."

"Use your spit. *Anything.* I need you inside me."

I feel a wet trail of something coat my hole. I don't know if it's his spit or paint, but I don't care. All I care about is the bliss that accompanies the slow steady pressure of him entering me.

"Still so tight for me," he rasps, plastering his bare front against my back, grinding his cock into me. "You aren't happy unless you have a big dick up your ass."

He's right. He's so *fucking* right. I tried to ignore it. I tried to push it aside. I tried to fight it.

But this is real. This is perfect. This is everything.

"Please, Noah," I groan, gasping when he manages to tilt my hips up and nail my prostate. "Yes! Right there! Yes, yes, yes!"

"You pissed me off, babe," he growls. "You tried to break things off with me. You tried to take this away from us."

"I'm sorry," I cry, hands scrambling for purchase on the table, his thrusts frantic and animalistic, all his anger pouring out as he fucks me. "Please, please, please don't stop."

"Does God give you this? Can God make you feel this way?"

"No!"

"Who fucks you the way you've always wanted? Who's the one you need to worship?"

"You!"

He uses one hand to angle my head toward his. He licks a long stripe against my parted lips, his tongue hot and possessive. "Don't you dare try to ruin this, Jarred. I'll fuck you a million times to remind you that *we're* right."

"Noah," I whine, my lips and my soul and my body aching and yearning and crumbling. "Noah, I need you."

He continues his relentless drilling of that magical spot and I'm coming all over the table, my cum mixing with the paint under my cock, drained of everything I have. I'm boneless as I feel him still inside of me, experience his cock swell, and hear his loud grunt as he comes.

"Oh, you're so fucking perfect," he murmurs, wrapping his arms around me and holding me close to his chest as he kisses the back of my head and pulls out.

"Noah," I rasp, feeling so exposed. I hug his arm to my chest and kiss all over his bare skin. "Baby…"

He helps me up and snickers when he sees my upper thighs, cock, and shirt are all covered in different shades of paint. He looks down at where my cum landed on his palette and smiles. "I'm going to make this a part of my painting and every time I see it, I'll be reminded that you're fucking *mine*."

I am his. Wholeheartedly. God…I can't even think of Him right now because nothing feels as right as now. The rightness of Noah gently redressing me, the certainty of how he kisses the corner of my slack mouth, and the certitude of the little whispered secrets he gives me.

"Think about it, babe, because I can't help it. I think I'd wait for you."

And my chest tightens. Despite how he may appear—filled with rage and frustration, swallowed by sarcastic anguish and vivid pain—he's so fucking patient.

I…I think I've been waiting for *him* forever.

But I don't get to tell him any of this when the door to the studio swings open. We bolt apart quickly, but the damage is done. Bryce walks in and his face is filled with nothing but confusion. I don't blame him. Noah and I are both covered in paint. Thankfully, we're both fully dressed—minus Noah's bare chest—but there's no realistic way to explain why I probably look freshly fucked and why there are red handprints all over my back.

"Bryce," I cough out, straightening up and stepping toward him. "Can I help you?"

Bryce blinks repeatedly and shakes his head in a daze. "I…no. I was just—Nothing."

And he walks away before I can stop him.

Suddenly, I can't breathe. I can't fucking breathe. My chest hurts and my vision is blurry. I can feel the tip of my fingers zap with something akin to electricity, and I've never been so aware of how heavy my tongue is and how dead my limbs are.

"Babe. Babe. Look at me."

My eyes zero in on Noah. His face is worried as he rubs his hands up and down my arms.

"Breathe, Jarred. It's okay."

"B-but Bryce…h-he…" I cut myself off with a loud heave. I feel like I'm going to throw up.

Noah shakes his head. "I'll take care of it. I promise. I'll handle it.

Please, just breathe with me." He places my hand over his chest. "Breathe with me, Jarred. In and out."

I follow the pattern of his breaths, leaning on him and wrapping my arms around his waist as I try to calm down. "Noah—"

"I'll take care of it, Jarred. I promise."

And all I can do is breathe. Breathe. Breathe and hold onto the promise that Noah will take care of it.

Take care of me.

CHAPTER 20
NOAH

I can't run fast enough.

I'm barreling through the camp, nearly knocking campers over in my haste to catch up to Bryce. I don't know where he went, and I don't know exactly what he's thinking. All I know is that Jarred is freaking out, and I'm about ready to do anything to make it all better.

With a sigh of relief, I spot Bryce by the chapel just talking to Joshua. Before I can think better of it or try to come up with some reasonable way to approach him, I'm marching up to him and yanking him away by the back of his polo.

"Bro, what the fuck!" Joshua yells, but he doesn't do anything to help his friend.

"We need to talk," I say to Bryce as I drag him away. I go to the first relatively private spot I see which is in the woods near the edge of the clearing. He tries to fight me as I take him there, but he's speechless. I think he might know better than to try and test me right now, especially with how pissed off I must look.

He finally finds his words when I shove him up against a tree, still holding onto the back of his collar as I move into his space. "Noah! What are you—"

"Shut up," I snap, digging my nails into the side of his neck, feeling his erratically pulsing heartbeat. "Why did you come to the studio?"

He gulps, straining to get out of my grip. "Sarah said she left her bracelet there, and I was going to check."

It sounds reasonable enough. Sarah, one of the younger elementary school campers was in that class earlier today, but I don't trust a single thing that comes out of Bryce's mouth. He could have been coming in there to fuck me with, God knows he's been itching for the chance since our last altercation.

"What did you see?" I ask, cutting to the chase. I just want to get to the bottom of what he saw. I want to establish where we're at. The way he blinks up at me seems clueless enough, but I know better than to fall for that act.

"I didn't see—"

"What did you *see*?"

His eyes widen and I fucking notice. I notice the little knowing flash in his beady eyes. So, that was an act. He was trying to play off being an oblivious idiot. Well, I'm not one of those and I know how to call bullshit. He's lying. This act isn't fooling me.

I know guys like Bryce. I was surrounded by them growing up in the privileged family I had. When they can't get something by sheer force of will, they'll resort to any method to get their way. Bryce has put a target on my back for a while now, and I can't help but wonder if it's because of more than just the beating I gave him.

I shift my fingers to close around the front of his throat and he gulps. "You and Jarred looked..."

He trails off and I press harder. "Finish your fucking sentence."

"You looked close."

I hide the way my breath hitches. It's confirmation of what I already knew, but I hate hearing it all the same. I shake my head, my jaw clenching and my molars grinding with each word. "That's where you're wrong. I want to set the record straight. All you saw was him helping me clean up after a session at the studio. He tripped and fell all over the paint. Right?"

"It's disgusting that you want me to believe that," he says. He gulps again when I wrap my other hand around his throat. "I could tell everyone."

"There's nothing to tell," I say.

"I think there is."

"Listen to me very carefully. You think what I did to you that first night was rough? It's not. Don't underestimate me. I will beat the living shit out of you and enjoy it if you even breathe a word of what you *think* you saw."

"You're awfully defensive right now," he notices, raising his eyebrows with something so close to fucking smugness that I want to punch right off him. "You're not making your situation any better."

Fuck, I'm really not. If there was going to be a doubt about what happened between Jarred and me in that studio, it's gone. But I already knew that. I already knew that this situation was shit because Bryce might be an idiot but he's not dumb. He saw what he saw. He saw my handprints around the front of Jarred's pants. He saw our kiss-swollen lips. He saw it all.

So, if I have to confirm even an ounce of it to get him to cooperate, I will. Because, scarily enough, I don't think there's anything I wouldn't do to protect Jarred.

I level him with my best stare, my lips curling into a snarl as his cheeks turn pink by the force of my hands. "Look me in the eyes right now. Think about the worst thing that could possibly happen to you. Not just bodily harm. Think about what would ruin you, break you, and destroy you. I will figure out what it is and make sure it happens. Don't test me."

It takes him a moment and, with a lot of difficulty, he nods. "I didn't see anything."

"Good. Now get the fuck out of my sight," I bark, shoving him onto the ground for good measure before stomping past him.

I leave him in the forest, flustered and slightly traumatized, just like I wanted. I head back to the art studio to look for Jarred, but he isn't there. I figure he's probably back at his cabin changing, and I itch to go search for him. It's not smart. Not after Bryce saw what he saw. I know everybody else knows nothing, but the burden of this secret feels extra heavy on my shoulders like weights dragging me down.

The day is almost impossible to get through but somehow, I manage. I go through the motions of the day—continuing with my second art session, supervising the afternoon swim at the lake, and facilitating the dining room line—but I think about Jarred the entire time. I don't spot him at any point during the day, and it makes me think that he's probably hiding out somewhere.

My heart clenches because he must be so scared.

Finally, once Kendall does her nightly checks, I sneak out of my cabin and head to his place. I knock on the door to his cabin, making sure to check no one is straggling around the most deserted clearing. When he doesn't answer, I knock again. With a huff, I continue to knock.

"Babe, it's just me," I say softly against the door and when I'm about to knock again, it finally opens.

Jarred looks *wrecked*.

His normally composed blond hair is all over the place. His dark brown eyes are bloodshot as if he's been crying. He's all twitchy and flustered as he rushes me into his cabin. Immediately, his hands are on my arms. "What happened?"

"I took care of it," I tell him, trying to soothe with my soft tone and even softer gaze. "I took care of it just like I told you I would."

He shakes his head as he worries the inside of his cheek. "But Bryce could still say something."

"He won't," I insist firmly. "If he does, which I doubt he will, I'll make sure everything is okay."

"You can't promise that," he says, his breaths coming in little uneven bursts. "He could still say something. Everybody would know. I would—"

"I won't let anything hurt you, Jarred," I say, cutting him off. I place my hands on his cheeks, rubbing my thumbs against his lower lip. "I mean it. Believe me."

It takes him a bit. More than a few minutes before he manages to calm down. He leans on me, placing his forehead against mine, his breath hot on my lips as he exhales shakily. "Thank you. Thank you. Thank you."

I revel in the way he sags against me. I want to take care of him. I want to comfort him. I want to be the person he trusts. I need to know that I have the power to make him feel better. Why? I'm not too sure, but it's a burning need inside me to make sure that he knows that he can put his faith in me. I won't let him down.

I want to protect him. Maybe that's just a quality of mine I never really knew I had until I came here. I want to shield his large body from anybody that would dare hurt him. He's...precious. He's kind, sweet, and trusting. He's a mended soul that just needs someone to be there for him.

However...

"Jarred, don't freak out but..."

He raises his head with a frown. "I don't think I like where this is going."

"What could be the worst thing that would happen if you came out?"

Instantly, he scrambles away from me. His eyes widen as he clutches at his chest. It looks like he's about to have a heart attack and at his age, I don't doubt that this would push him right over the edge if he let it. "So, you do think he's going to say something."

"No, that's not what I'm saying," I say with a shake of my head. "I'm just wondering...what if?"

What if Bryce actually said something? What if I failed? What really could be the worst thing that could happen? I'm not pushing Jarred to come out, but he would be free, wouldn't he? He wouldn't have to hide. He wouldn't have to feel ashamed. He wouldn't have to be terrified of himself. In the worst-case scenario, we could get through it.

Maybe together.

But that's not where his head is. He looks like I've just slapped him. He's shaking his head wildly, pacing in front of me as his nails scratch at his wrists. "My life would be ruined. This camp and everything I've worked for...gone. That can't happen. It can never happen."

Something inside me crumbles a bit. I know it might be ridiculous to think this, especially because it's only been less than two months, but I could picture this being more. Maybe not right away, maybe not now, but it could be if we let it.

But he's right. There's no future here. His life is dedicated to the person he tells everyone else he is. His future is contingent on the lies and shame he carries, and it's a future I'm not allowed to be a part of.

But fuck it all because I'm going to enjoy every last second I get with him. No matter what. I've had a taste of him. I've had these stolen moments. I've seen how…amazing it all is with him.

I'll cherish and guard it with everything I have. Even if it means knowing this will end.

"Okay, it was just a question," I whisper, approaching him steadily as I take hold of both his hands. "None of that is going to happen."

He nods and chews at the bottom of his lip. He glances up at me through his lashes, so vulnerably broken it makes my insides curl. "Can you…can you stay here with me tonight?"

I smile at him, leaning forward to press the barest of kisses against his lips. "Of course."

No more words are exchanged as we start to undress. He's never asked me to stay the night before. After we fuck, it's always a rush to make sure I'm gone before the sun goes up, but I know he needs this tonight. Fuck, maybe I do too. Maybe I just need to feel close to him.

I slide under the covers, and he automatically turns on his side away from me. I go to do the same until he reaches back and wraps my arm around his waist. I sigh contently as I snuggle into his back, my nose trailing against the back of his neck. Neither of us goes to sleep right away. We just lay there in each other's arms, breathing each other in, and taking a quiet moment to relish in this reprieve.

And maybe, like me, he's wondering why this feels as right as it does.

CHAPTER 21
NOAH

"Hey, Noah. Can I talk to you?"

I raise my pierced brow, turning away from the bonfire Kendall, Patrick, and I are sitting around to see Ian standing behind us. I groan. This is supposed to be counselor time. It's close to lights out, and Ian should be in his bunk already.

I suck in a long deep breath, pressing my lips together as I kill my cigarette. "Sure. What's up, buddy?"

Ian looks at Kendall and Patrick, his eyes wide and his freckle-covered cheeks pink as he looks back at me. "In private?"

I share a look with Kendall and Patrick, all of us seem just slightly weirded out and wary. Regardless, I can sense something is up. "Sure."

I get up off the log I'm sitting on and gesture for Ian to follow me. We're not far from the lake, so I take him just a little bit away from the other counselors. "What's this about?"

Ian's fingers twitch as he picks at his shirt. "I still haven't heard back from my parents."

"*Dude*," I groan, running my hand down my face. "For the last time, I told you—"

"I want to go home."

I rear my head back a little. This is the first camper who's expressed not wanting to be here. Even though this might not be my thing, everyone else has seemed really happy so far. I take a closer look at Ian —his nervous little tell and his shaky fingers—and my blood runs cold. "Why? Is anyone giving you trouble?"

"No, not at all," he says quickly with a shake of his head, but I don't know if I believe him. Sure, the kids here are all relatively good, but there are kids like Bryce in the making that might be giving him shit. "I just don't belong here."

"Why's that?"

"I think…when you gave ministry…I realized…"

I take a soft step toward him and place my hand reassuringly on his shoulder. "Come on, kid. Spit it out."

"I'm gay!" he shouts, blurting it out so loudly and covering his mouth with a cringe when he realizes it.

I nod slowly. I'm not really too sure what to do. "Thank you for telling me that," I say. "Is that why you want to go home?"

"I saw the way the other campers reacted when you came out," he says nervously. "What if they find out about me?"

For a second, I'm angry. I'm angry that people like Jarred, Patrick, and Ian have to be so afraid to come out. But then I turn compassionate. I can see that it's killing this kid, wrecking him from the inside out, and his fellow campers' reaction to my coming out probably doesn't help the situation.

I shake my head. "They won't unless you want them to. What are you feeling right now?"

"Wrong. Scared." His lips tremble as tears spring from his eyes. "Afraid that God will punish me."

I let out a deep sigh. Poor kid. I hate this. I hate that anyone has to feel this way. "A lot of people that were raised in the church feel that way when they come out."

"How did you move past it?"

I don't know why, but I never felt like this when I came out. Well, I haven't officially come out to my parents, but I never felt the need to. I'm out at school—I don't try to hide my attraction to the men I pick up —but I'm surprisingly good at brushing away all the homophobic shit that's sometimes thrown at me.

Even though I was raised in the church, I've never actually been afraid of God.

"I..." I shrug and tell him the honest truth. "I realized that if God was real, he'd love me for me, I guess."

He cocks his head to the side, wiping at his tears. "So...so, God isn't real?"

"I didn't say that. Only you know what you believe," I say firmly. I'm not in the business of trying to manipulate people into believing what I believe. That's not cool. Kids are impressionable and Ian needs to know that he needs to come to his own conclusion. "If you choose to believe in God, believe in the version you want to believe in, but don't let anyone tell you that there's something wrong with you."

Ian nods slowly. He sniffles a bit, but I can tell that he's taking my words seriously. In such a small voice, and with a shaky smile, he speaks. "Thanks, Noah."

"Anytime," I say sincerely. I know I can be a dick sometimes to the kids, but I guess I genuinely care what happens to them. "You still want to call your parents? I don't have reception, but I can sneak you into Jarred's office."

He chuckles at that and shakes his head. "No, I...I think I'll stay for a little bit longer."

"I'm serious, Ian. Whenever you need to talk, I'm here."

Ian gives me another tentative smile. "I will. I should get back though. We're kinda throwing a slumber party in cabin ten."

I snort at his so-called rebellion. The kids aren't allowed to be out of their assigned bunks, but I won't say shit. I ruffle his hair a little as I shove him away from me playfully. "Knock yourself out, kid."

I don't go back to the bonfire after he leaves. I can't. All I can do is sit and think about what just happened. I pull out a joint from my back pocket and light up, thinking about just how fucked up the world is.

Jarred wanted to know why I'm so angry? *This* is why. Ian's a good kid, but I have no doubt some of the campers would turn on him if they found out he's gay. I think about the kid I barely knew who killed himself and the life he could have lived. So, yeah, I don't believe in God. Why believe in something that would just let this shit slide?

I don't realize how long I've been out here until Jarred appears beside me. I glance down at my watch and see that it's way past lights out and after I would have come to his cabin. Kendall's going to give me shit for missing bunk checks.

"I was wondering where you were," he says with an easy smile but then he frowns and wrinkles his nose when he sees the half-smoked joint. "Marijuana? Seriously?"

I chuckle, my high at its perfect peak. "It's called weed, grandpa."

"Don't remind me that I'm two decades older than you," he says, but I don't need the reminder when he lets out a loud groan as he sits down beside me. "It makes me feel like a creep."

"Nah, you're not creepy at all," I say, smacking a kiss against his cheek. When I see him eyeing the joint, I hold it out to him. "You want some?"

He blushes. "I've never smoked before."

"No pressure," I shrug, taking a quick hit. "You don't have to if you don't want to."

He stares at the joint for a minute longer and, with resolute determination, takes it from me. My eyes widen at the deep hit he takes before I even have the chance to warn him to take it easy. He lets out a loud cacophony of coughs and painful wheezes that make tears spring in his eyes. "What the fuck!"

"Shit, I love it when you curse," I laugh, rubbing his back to help him through his fit. "You should have let me warn you first."

"I can handle it," he says, but his red face and his bloodshot eyes tell me that I'd better keep the weed away from him.

"Sure, babe," I say softly, reaching for his hand. When he laces his fingers with mine, easily leaning against my side and resting his head on my shoulder, I let out a sigh of peace.

It's nice. I don't feel like I need to fill the silence with him. We just sit there together, enjoying the dark stillness, looking at the moon's reflection on the lake.

"Want to go for a swim?" I ask him after a while, tugging on his hand to get his attention.

He furrows his brows at me and cocks his head to the side. "This late?"

"Sure," I say, standing up as I kill the joint. "Why the fuck not?"

When I start stripping, his eyes widen. He looks around us wildly and tries to throw my clothes back at me. "What are you doing?"

"Skinny dipping," I laugh, chucking my clothes right back at him.

"Anybody could see," he hisses, once again checking the very isolated area around us. He's been less wary since the whole Bryce situation happened a few days ago, but I can tell he's paranoid. I'm certain there's no one out here. He should know I'd never put him in that kind of position.

"Everybody is in their bunks," I assure him. I take a step away from him and don't miss the way his eyes glaze over as they track my figure. Just to give him a little show, I run my hand down my stomach to my half-hard cock and give it a tug. "You coming, grandpa?"

He grits his teeth as he stands, roughly pulling off his shirt with a scowl. "I don't know when this grandpa thing started, but it needs to stop."

"Sorry, babe. You're just too cute when you're flustered," I tease, slapping his bare ass when he finishes stripping. I grab his hand and pull him toward the lake. "Let's go."

He comes—albeit hesitantly—and relaxes once we're hidden in the water. For his benefit, I lead us to a part of the lake that's shielded by a big ass rock. It's all the way on the other side of where the cabins are, so I'm confident no one is going to see us.

"Mm, come here," I mumble, pulling his wet figure against me as I slot my mouth over his.

Despite his wariness, his hot mouth is hungry and sloppy for me. We kiss lazily, slowly nipping at each other's lips, tracing each other's tongues with our own, fucking smoothly with our mouths as our cocks grow hard. When he wraps those thick thighs around my waist, there's nothing more I want than to sink into that tight hole of his, but I refrain. There's no lube and there's no way I'm fucking him in the water where I could hurt him. Regardless, I do bring my fingers behind him and tease that little asshole a bit, smiling against his lips when he groans.

He reaches up with one hand to play with one of my nipple piercings I know he loves. He won't say it, but he's a kinky fuck. The dirtier the better for him. Fuck, I love it when he—

"Holy shit!"

Jarred tears himself away from me at my shout, looking around wildly at my panic. "What? Did you see someone?"

"No. I—" I let out a deep shudder as my heart races. "A fish just tried to swim up my ass!"

He blinks at me. "What?"

"You heard me! Fuck! Stop laughing!" I say, but I'm laughing along with him. I can't help it. "Motherfucking handsy-ass fish. He'll be lucky if I don't catch him and make him my dinner."

"You're cute when you're flustered," he says, throwing my previous words right back at me as he pinches my cheeks.

I half-heartedly slap his hand away. "Fuck you."

"Do you want to?" he teases, swimming back up to me, his hand firmly planted and rubbing soothing circles on my ass. "We could go back to my cabin."

Something hits me at this moment. I have no idea why or where it came from, but it's pain. It's a deep, unflinching, irrevocable kind of torment. It's out of the blue but that doesn't make it hurt any less.

"What are we doing, Jarred?"

"I thought you were going to put that cock in my ass."

"I mean...us."

It's something that I've wondered about that I haven't wanted to bring up. I've been thinking about it for these last few days since Jarred confirmed that there never could really be an *us*. I thought I was fine with it. But tonight, under the moonlight, smiling and laughing, I can't help but admit that I might not be.

Because I want this. I want this all the time. I'm falling for this generous mess of a man, and I don't know what to do about it. I'm too weak to pull away from him, but I don't know if I'm strong enough to see this through.

He's hesitant as his hand stills. "What about us?"

"It's halfway through the summer," I say gently, afraid that I'll scare him off. "What are we going to do when it's over?"

"I..." His cheeks lose their color. He tries to swim away from me, but I hold him tight, locking my legs around his thighs to keep him pressed against me. "I hadn't thought of that."

"Well, think about it," I say, a little firmer this time, a little bit tinted with my own pathetic insecurities. I hate to pressure him, but I need to know. "Jarred."

"I don't know, Noah..." He trails off and pinches his brows together, looking so beautifully torn and tragically fragile. "I don't know what to do."

"Do you want this to end?"

"No," he rushes out. Now he does plant his hands on both of my cheeks, rubbing my lip piercing, his eyes wide with terror. "No. I don't."

"Me neither." I shudder at the thought of a future without him, at how attached I've gotten already. "How would that work?"

"UNC is only a few hours away. Maybe you could come and visit? Texting is a thing, even though I'm not that good at it."

I'm too somber to point out that his age is the cause of that. "I mean..."

"What?"

It takes everything in me to breathe the following words. I hate how vulnerable it makes me sound. I'm supposed to be the strong one. I'm supposed to be the one that comforts him. I'm supposed to be the one that shields him from the ugliness of the world, but I feel like all that is crumbling at the pleading look in his eyes. "Am I going to be your dirty secret?"

"Noah," he sighs, pressing a kiss to my nose as he shuts his eyes. "Baby..."

"I'm not going to force you to come out," I state, and I mean it. "But I don't want to hide. How is that going to work when you're running this camp?"

He swallows audibly. "I can't come out."

"I know."

"It would ruin the camp."

"I know that too."

"We can make it work," he nearly begs, and I swear I see tears in his bloodshot eyes. "Can you settle for that now?"

"Yeah, I can," I say, but the words taste bitter on my tongue. And because I can't handle this anymore, I change the subject. "How about we go back to your cabin and fuck?"

He looks so relieved to be in a place that's familiar to us, away from the ugly truth that awaits us in a few short weeks. "That sounds good. Will you...will you use the toy again?"

I laugh—genuine now—and kiss the tip of his nose. "That greedy asshole likes being stuffed?"

He blushes and tries to avert his gaze. "Yes."

"Your wish is my command, babe."

And it is. There's no other option but to cave to his every whim. I can't leave him, and he can't come out. I've...trapped myself in this endless cycle of pain. But it's pure ecstasy. It's the sweetest kind of torture that I'd let tear me limb from limb as long as it was he who put me back together again.

Maybe this is what Father Matteo meant when he said that we have to make sacrifices for the ones we love. I'm so close to love, so close to being blindly connected to Jarred forever, and I think I'm ready to sacrifice just about anything.

Even my worth.

CHAPTER 22
JARRED

We walk back to my cabin without a word. Noah seems pensive and quiet, and I can't lie and say it doesn't make me nervous. But the steady pressure of our fingers intertwined—walking hand in hand through the forest—makes those nerves settle. Excitement takes its place as we reach and enter my cabin.

I'm ready for all the filthy things he's going to do with me. I want him and that dildo inside of me again. After our conversation in the lake, his silent and vulnerable plea to not be my secret, I think we need this.

I turn to him—a smirk on my face—and stop when I see the look on his. Those beautiful hazel eyes are filled with something foreign, almost hesitant, showing no signs of the sinful carnage I was expecting.

"Noah?" I question, taking a step toward him and reaching for his hand. "Is everything okay?"

I start to panic a bit. Maybe our conversation by the lake really did get to him. Maybe he just played off his true emotions to appease me. Maybe he's rethinking everything we're doing, knowing that he could do better than a forty-five-year-old man who can't give him more than this.

But then he kisses me. It's...sweet and gentle. It's like he's never kissed me before. It's like the first kiss we should have had, soft and almost youthful in its inexperience.

"Jarred," he whispers against my lips, reaching for the hem of my shirt. "Jarred…"

I wait for him to say something else, but he doesn't. He just starts slowly undressing me, taking his time, his fingers tracing every inch of me as he lays me down on the bed. Once I'm naked and ready for him, he doesn't follow suit. Noah's become acquainted with my cabin and, for some reason, he goes straight to my closet. I stare at him quizzically as he starts pulling out various candles. I'm not too sure how he knows they were there. I keep them in case we get a power outage like we have in the past. He must have noticed them one day as I was getting dressed.

My confusion doesn't go away as he wordlessly starts lighting them, placing them in every corner of the cabin until the only thing illuminating the dark are flickering flames painting shadows across the walls.

"What's happening?" I ask, but he ignores me as he starts undressing. He slips out of his shirt, his beautiful figure on display, his nipple piercings shining under the candlelight. He continues until he's naked, and I take a moment to soak it all in.

He looks like a god. He looks like the perfect picture of youth—covered in piercings, tone and lean, filled with so much life—and I wonder for a split second what he must see in me to choose me.

"Jarred," he says again, falling to his knees in front of the bed, his magical hands rubbing up and down my calves. "Let me."

I'm not too sure what he's asking permission for, but I nod. Noah can do anything to me. He can treat me like his whore and spit in my mouth and slap my ass until it's numb.

But that's not what he does.

He starts at my ankles, kissing each one, his lips smooth against my skin. His tongue traces a path up my calf, paying special attention to the area behind my knee, and it makes me erupt in goosebumps. He leans up, takes my cock in his hands, and kisses the tip. His tongue swipes out to taste my precum, but it's not as aggressive and animalistic as it usually is.

"The first time I saw you, I knew I wanted you," he whispers against my cock, rubbing it against his cheek in something akin to admiration. "When I saw how scared you were about what you wanted, I wanted to protect you."

I gulp audibly. "Noah…"

"You are…" He pauses as he crawls up my body, sucking one nipple into his hot mouth, moaning around the peak. "I don't even know if I can put it into words."

I'm nothing but putty in his hands, under his tongue, against his body. "Can you try?"

He looks up at me, smiling like…like I mean everything to him. "I've told you you're perfect, but I don't think you understand what I mean by that. It's not just this gorgeous body." He presses his chest against mine and buries his face in my neck. "Your soul, Jarred. Babe, your soul is so perfect. It's so pure. It's meant for me."

And I can feel that it is. I feel the tugging, the pull, the all-consuming connection I have with him right now. He slinks back down my body, gently pushing my legs apart and against my chest. He doesn't need to tell me what to do. I wrap my arms around the back of my thighs and open up to him. He stares at my hole with reverence, closing his eyes and he leans forward and practically inhales me. I can't find it in me to be sheepish or embarrassed because of how content he looks.

He kisses my hole. Once, twice, three times before his tongue laps at it. He sucks, he kisses, he caresses until he slowly works his tongue inside of me. I close my eyes and just bask in it. Bask in his attention, his care, his admiration. But I grow impatient and needy. I want him. I want him to fuck me because this feels like too much.

"Noah," I whine breathlessly, letting go of my thighs, so I can reach for his shoulders. "Please…"

"Not yet, babe," he says against my hole, working a wet finger in me. "I need this."

I don't know what he means by that. I can't begin to understand what's going on in his head. But when he slides three fingers into me at once, stretching my tight hole, I lose all reason. What his motivations are doesn't matter at the moment. All that matters is *this*.

Finally, he takes mercy on me. He licks his wet lips, almost as if trying to memorize my taste as he reaches for the lube in my nightstand. He strokes himself a few times but doesn't immediately plunge in. Instead, he lays down beside me. I'm confused yet again. This is supposed to lead to mind-blowing sex, but he doesn't seem to be in a rush.

He lays on his side and moves me over until I'm mimicking his position. He takes my leg and hitches it around his waist, bending it until it's practically tucked under his armpit. I furrow my brows at him, but he only pecks my nose.

"I want it like this," he says, lining up against my hole before pushing in. I groan and he smiles, tracing one finger down my nose as he seats himself fully inside me. "I need to look at you, babe."

I nod dumbly because now that he's inside of me, all is right. I'm pliant and moveable as he manages to get my arms around his neck. He presses his forehead against mine and brushes his nose across my cheek. "Open your eyes, Jarred. Watch me."

I follow his command because there's no way I can't. What I see shocks me. I gasp as he slowly thrusts in and out of me, his murmured groans stirring something inside of me. His eyes—those beautiful hazel eyes—are like windows into his soul. I can see everything he's feeling. He's bared to me, vulnerable for me, and it makes me want to cry. Not because it's upsetting or I'm against what's happening but because he's trusting me with this part of himself.

"I think you're it for me, babe," he murmurs against my lips, one hand brushing the hair away from my face. "I can be whatever you need me to be."

This time tears do spring in my eyes. "Baby, I don't—"

His hand wanders from my hair, down my chest, wrapping around my cock. "Nice and slow. Fucking you like this. Do you like it?"

"Yes," I groan, closing my eyes briefly when his cock drags against my sensitive walls. "I've never felt this before."

"Tell me what you feel."

"Seen."

"What else, babe? Give me more." He grunts as he pulls all the way out before slowly sliding back in. "Give me everything."

I gulp and nod, lying on my back as he hovers over me. He places one hand on my heart, the other still stroking my cock. "Complete. I feel complete."

"I'll always make you feel like that," he says. "I'll be your dirty secret. Just don't take this away from me."

"Never," I say desperately, leaning up so I can kiss him. I pour everything I have, everything I can give into this kiss. I want him to know how deeply I feel for him. I need him to know that despite all the obstacles we face, I never want to let him go. "I'll always want to belong to you."

Noah likes this. He moans low in his throat and finally gives me what I had been expecting. He doesn't need any toys or any filthy words to make me come. His beautiful torture is enough, that tenderness gets me there. It fills me slowly, curling around in my gut, like molten lava dripping down a volcano. I come on a gasp, coating his hand in my cum, shaking and shuddering as I feel him fill me up.

And I wish I could be whatever he needs me to be, but I can't. Not yet. And my heart stings because a brutally cruel thought crosses my head and tears at my heart.

Maybe not ever.

CHAPTER 23
JARRED

I try to even out my breath. It's hard to control the rapid beating of my heart and the way my palms sweat. I never thought I would do this. I never thought I'd be capable of it, but I have to.

I'm going to tell Father Matteo about me and Noah.

It might be sheer insanity that's driving me to do this, but Noah makes me crazy in all the best ways. The conversation I had with him by the lake a few days ago was illuminating. I didn't realize how terror-stricken I would be at the thought of my life without him. It didn't help that when we got back to my cabin, he...he fucked me like he loved me. Slow, gentle, smooth. Only soft praised whispers fell from his normally dirty tongue, and it entranced me.

I don't want Noah to have to hide. I couldn't stand the almost vulnerably heartbroken look on Noah's face when he asked me about us.

I can't come out. I *can't* but maybe Father Matteo can give me some guidance. I just need to know what to do.

I steel myself and walk into the chapel. I have to do this. I have to do this for Noah. I have to do it for us. I need to tell someone about all these feelings that are swirling around in my head, my heart, my gut, my fucking everywhere.

I see Father Matteo standing at the front of the chapel, sorting through the vigil candles he keeps in the corner. I suck in a deep breath as I approach him, and my legs feel numb. I clear my throat once to get his attention. "Hey, Matteo. Do you have time to talk?"

Father Matteo raises his brows at me, probably cautious because I never refer to him like that. "As your priest or your friend?"

"Both. I could…"

I trip over my own words. I can't do this. I can't—

Noah. Noah. Noah.

"I have something to say," I finish, gulping harshly.

He nods. "Let's step into my office."

"Can we do it in here?" I ask quickly, gesturing at the pews. "I kind of want Him to hear it too."

"If that's what you want," he says, following suit as I take a seat on the front pew. He cocks his head to the side as he places a gentle hand on my back. "Are you okay? You look like you're going to vomit."

That's not far from the truth. I have so many things running through my mind. My father, the bastard, beating me into heterosexual submission. The porn I was forced to watch. The constant hours he made me spend on my knees begging for God's mercy.

Noah. Noah. Noah.

But that thought alone rings through all the fog.

"I have been battling something for a while now," I begin, clasping my hands in front of me, eyes locked on the crucifix just above the altar. "I wasn't going to say anything or act on it because it was wrong, but I think the time has come for me to be honest with myself and with God."

"Is this about the camp counselor you're attracted to?" he asks.

I nod shakily. "Yes."

"Is it about Noah?"

I think my heart actually skips a beat. I whip my head at him, my mouth drawn open in sheer horror as I stare at his knowing gaze. "Wait, you know about him? How?"

"Bragging is frowned upon by the church, but I'm smart," he says with a small shrug of one shoulder. "I've seen the way you've looked at him during mass."

"Do you think anybody else noticed?" I ask, suddenly paranoid that my feelings for Noah have been broadcasted for the world to see this entire time.

"You're my friend, Jarred," he chuckles softly, patting my back. "I've known you for ten years. I don't think others know you as well as I do."

"Okay. Good," I breathe, calming down just a bit. "That's good."

Father Matteo waits for a second, probably for me to collect my bearings before he speaks again. "So, you and Noah."

"We're together."

He nods carefully and raises his hands in confusion. "So, what's the problem?"

"What do you mean what's the problem?" I ask with wide eyes, staring at him in shock. "That's the problem. I'm..."

But my breathing has picked up again. *God* is watching. I wanted Him to but the weight of his presence around me feels suffocating. I tug at the collar of my polo, my spit suddenly drying up, my tongue heavy and fumbling in my mouth.

Father Matteo's patient as he waits for me to calm down again. "It's okay to say it."

This is it. These are the words that have been so hard to say. The ones that have been keeping me up at night. The ones that I wanted so badly to not be true, but they are.

"I'm gay."

It feels...strange. Maybe not the sweet relief some people claim they feel when they speak the truth, but it's...lighter, maybe? Perhaps, the heavy feeling in my chest has eased just a tad. My fingers still zap with little tremors and my feet keep tapping away at the faded carpet, but I'm still alive. God hasn't smitten me where I sit.

Father Matteo smiles, bright and shiny as if I didn't just confess a heavy sin in His house. "Thank you for telling me."

"What? You're not going to tell me I'm going straight to hell for it?" I ask, preparing to hear all the foul things my father said. All the taunts. *Pansy. Cocksucker.* All those horribly poisonous words that marked me as *wrong*.

"Now, why would I say that?" he asks, leaning back on the pew as he clasps his hands over his stomach, looking at me with intrigue.

I fumble for an answer that should be so obvious to him. "Because it's…"

"Wrong? Disgusting? Immoral? Do you truly believe that, Jarred?"

"Yes, I mean, no." I correct myself. "I used to. Or I do. It's complicated."

"Do you want me to tell you you're going to burn in hell?" he questions, tipping his head toward the altar. "Do you want me to say that God hates you now?"

"Doesn't he?" I ask, my voice small as I stare at His likeness hanging right in front of me.

"Why would he? God loves all his people. Despite what you think, his love isn't contingent on your sexuality."

"You're a priest," I gasp, shaking my head at the absurdity of it all. "How can you say that?"

"Because I've lived," he puts it simply. "Because I've seen things. Because I believe that the gospel was written by man and man makes mistakes."

Mistakes. That's what I thought Noah was at first. One terribly inappropriate and corrupting mistake. I fought my hardest to resist him, I really did, but it was futile in the end. He wrapped me in his loving embrace, he held me close, he shielded me from everything, and he took me as I am.

I think that's all I've ever wanted. It's what I thought God could give me if I played straight. It's what I couldn't find in Jenny. I just wanted someone to want me for me, to accept me, to look at me and not think there was something dirty or immoral about me.

I think Noah's always wanted that too. I think that's why we clicked so well, drawn together like moths to a burning flame, as easily as the wind carries dusk's promises across the air.

"I think I love him," I admit quietly, looking at Father Matteo who's still smiling. I think I'm still in shock that he's not cringing and grabbing at his crucifix.

"Isn't that a bit too soon?" he jokes, and I know he's only teasing.

"That's why I said *think*. I want to see where this will go with him, but I don't know how I can live the life I live while being gay. Doesn't that mean I'm not catholic?"

He clicks his tongue in consideration. "That's a tricky one, and I don't have an answer for you. Technically, you're not, but you can still believe in God and love Him without being catholic. Ultimately, it's your life, Jarred. You need to do what's best for you."

But I still don't know what that is. I still don't know what the right choice is. I've told Father Matteo, but that's because I wanted God to know. I wanted to see how I would feel. Clarity isn't something I've gotten today. I want Noah. I want my life. I want God but is it even possible to have it all?

"Choose happiness, Jarred," Father Matteo says. "That's all God wants from you."

But if that's true then why is the choice between God and Noah this hard?

CHAPTER 24
NOAH

I run my hand through my wet hair, cursing with humor as I head back to camp from lifeguard duty. I hadn't been expecting to be pushed into the lake by a devious Patrick and Ian, but I can't help but find it funny. Those two little shits are definitely going to pay for that later.

As I turn the corner, somebody takes ahold of my arm, yanking my unprepared body into the rickety toolshed just at the exit of the woods. I brace myself for whatever it is, my heart thrumming in my chest when I think it might be Bryce being an idiot and trying to go another round. When I regain my senses after being pushed against the wall, I'm caught off guard when a pair of strong firm lips land on mine.

"Woah!" I say, blinking back my surprise as Jarred plants another kiss on my lips. "What was that?"

Jarred laughs, looking way too amused at catching me unready. He digs his fingers into my wet hair, grinding his hips against my damp trunks. "What? I can't kiss my boyfriend?"

"Boyfriend, huh?" I say, a wide grin splitting my face at the word. "When did that happen?"

He nips at the skin of my neck with loving attention. "I told Father Matteo about us."

"What—Jarred," I say, pushing him back at the bomb he just

dropped. My eyes widen as my jaw goes slack. "What do you mean? What did he say?"

Instead of looking how I expect after a confession like that—terrified and unsure—Jarred just looks so fucking happy. "He said it's okay. We're okay, baby."

Even though I'm happy for him, and even though I should be over the moon at this hallmark we've passed, I can't help but still feel a little pang of bitterness in my chest. "I wish you would have come to that conclusion on your own."

It's not that I'm not proud of him, I am, but needing someone else's approval for our relationship doesn't mean everything is okay. Jarred's smile drops a bit as his lips freeze on my neck. I can feel the whisper of doubt creeping in again, the hidden shame hanging thick between us. "I'm...I'm getting there."

I sigh and palm the back of his head. I roll my forehead against his as I kiss the tip of his nose. "I know, babe. I'm proud of you. I really am. This is a step in the right direction."

"I was thinking we could celebrate."

"Fuck yeah, we are. Tonight I'll bring by the dildo and we can—"

"No," he rushes out, assaulting my lips yet again with another toe-curling kiss. "No. I can't wait. *Now*. I want you now."

I look around the toolshed. This isn't exactly the spot I want to fuck him in, especially when there are hundreds of campers right on the other side of the very thin door. I bite at my bottom lip.

Typically, I'm the one who's pushing him to get out there and be a little bit more adventurous, but I'm cautious. Jarred doesn't seem to care. He's reaching down and palming my soft cock, bringing it to life with his easy and confident strokes. I can admit that this change in him is really turning me the fuck on.

"Okay," I breathe, my control slipping when he dips his hand into my trunks. "Okay. Let's go back to your cabin."

It's comical how quickly he's rushing out of the toolshed with me right on his heels. He's made me desperate for him, and I can't wait to sink into that tight hole. We're running through the camp like a couple of horny teenagers, giggling and laughing the entire way as we try to keep at the edge of the clearing and out of sight. We manage to make it to the cabin undetected and the second we're in, I'm pouncing at him.

I crash my lips against his, his tongue spearing into my mouth without any grace or delicacy. He's fucking my mouth with ravenous enthusiasm, already pulling down my trunks and falling to his knees in front of me. When he takes my cock in his mouth, my eyes roll to the back of my head. He's gotten a lot better at sucking me off, but in truth, he's always been perfect. Looking down at him, I can't help but feel my chest swell with affection—tender affection—and I realize I want to do something different today.

"I want you to fuck me."

Jarred's head snaps up to mine, my cock slipping from his mouth as his jaw drops. "You…what?"

"I want you to fuck me," I repeat, helping him onto his feet as I reach for his belt and slip his underwear and pants down to his ankles. "I want to feel you inside of me. I want that beautiful cock in my ass."

"I thought you might not want that," he says, reaching up to rub my shoulders. "I thought maybe—"

"That since I've been fucking you, I don't like to be the one on the other end?"

"Well, yeah."

"I prefer topping, but I'm vers," I admit, thinking back to the few times I've bottomed. It's always been…okay, and I definitely like being on top more, but it's different with Jarred. Everything is. "I want to be close to you. I want…I want to do it all with you."

He smiles sweetly. "I want that too, baby. How do I do this?"

"Just like when I do it to you," I say with a shrug, already helping him out of his polo. "Prep first, lots of lube, patience, and then all the good stuff."

"Can you lean over the bed?"

I chuckle, not making fun of him but finding his inexperience adorable. "You don't have to ask."

"Okay," he says, but he still looks very unsure, his fingers twitching restlessly at his sides.

"Are you nervous?" I ask softly, cupping his face. "We don't have to do this if you don't—"

"No, I want this," he says adamantly. "I'm just…I want it to be good for you."

My heart yet again melts for him. "It's you, Jarred. Anything you do to me is good. I promise."

It takes him a second, but he nods. He points at the bed, his fingers still trembling, but determination in his eyes. "Okay. Lean over the bed."

I smirk. His being in charge is kind of hot. I do exactly what he demands, leaning over the bed and spreading my ass cheeks for good measure. He rummages through the drawer for lube, and I can hear the sharp breath he sucks in, and I close my eyes in sweet pleasure as his slick finger ghosts over my hole.

"It's…it's beautiful. You're so beautiful, baby." He carefully pushes one thick finger in, twirling it inside of me, humming as he does. "You're so tight. It's so warm."

"It's all for you," I breathe, adjusting to the slight sting of being penetrated after so long without it.

"You're mine?"

The tone of his voice—reverent and adoring—makes me look over my shoulder. He's slipping a second finger in, but his eyes are on me. They're wide and soft, the caramel highlights in them sparkling as he gives me a shaky smile.

"Yeah," I whisper, reaching back to grab his free hand. "I'm yours."

"No matter what?"

My voice gets caught in my throat. I can't believe that we're here. I'm not even too sure when it happened. I'm not too sure when I realized I would give anything up for him, do anything for him, be anything he needs me to be. It feels like it happened slowly, so unnoticeable that I didn't pick up on it. He's a beautiful soul, inside and out, and something in him calls to me in a way nobody else ever has.

"I promise," I say, groaning when he slides a second finger in. "No matter what."

I'll take anything from him. Anything he throws at me, I'll happily accept. I'll see him through his turmoil, I'll be there for him if he falls, and I'll wait patiently for the day we can have our happy ever after.

Because he's worth it.

"I want your cock," I say through a rough swallow, crawling up onto the bed and flipping onto my back. I want to see him when he enters me for the first time. My mouth drops open with hunger at the way he's lubing up that thick cock, coating it with more slickness than needed, but I appreciate it.

He slinks up my body, pausing to trail kisses up my figure as he does. He nips at my hip, rubs his nose against my happy trail, and graces my nipples with his attention before kissing me. I'm so distracted, I barely feel it when he pushes into me and takes my breath away. It's unlike anything I've ever experienced. Where I've been tense with other partners who've done this to me, I'm so receptive to him. I swallow him up eagerly, only letting out one pained groan when he bottoms out.

"How does it feel?" he whispers against my lips, taking my cock in his hand with slow strokes.

"It's a bit tender, but it'll pass," I admit. I wrap my legs around his waist and urge him deeper inside me. "Go ahead and fuck me, babe. I'm dying for it."

He gives me another breathless smile as he begins thrusting at an agonizingly deliberate pace. It's like he wants to feel every spot, experience every unhurried drag of his cock, and relish in this moment the way I am.

"Oh my fuck...*Jarred*," I moan, clutching at his shoulders as I kiss his neck. "You feel so good filling me up."

"You feel amazing," he says, his voice husky and tight with tension. "Can I go faster?"

"*Fuck yes...*"

He picks up his pace, but he's impaling me with affectionate thrusts. He kisses everywhere he can reach on my face before burying his face in my neck. I can feel his rough grunts, his trembling breaths, his...love, maybe?

"Come," I say, realizing that my balls are drawing tight way too soon. I want this to last longer, but this moment is just too perfect. His reverence is just too sweet. His cock is just too good. It's all dragging me closer and closer to the edge. "Come, babe. I can't...I can't hold it."

He doesn't help the matter when he takes my cock in his hand again, matching each stroke with the snap of his hips. He must feel the same sensation I do because only a few moments later, and he's filling me with his cum. At the feel of it overflowing inside of me and trickling down my ass cheeks, I follow along with him.

He holds me tight in the aftermath, not pulling out, resting his weight comfortingly on top of me. "Thank you for doing that for me."

I smile as I kiss his sweaty temple. "What do you think?"

"I think I like bottoming better," he confesses after a moment of hesitation. He looks up at me, a sexy smirk pulling his lips. "But I'd do that again in a heartbeat. Maybe make it last longer."

I laugh along with him, only wincing once when he pulls out. We're a sweaty mess of tangled limbs when he pulls me up to his chest, his never-ending kisses to the top of my head doing something to me. It makes me so vulnerable, and I can't keep it in my thoughts because with every act of care, the truth bubbles to the surface. "Is it too soon to love you?"

His lips still on the top of my head. I can feel the heavy breaths he's letting out, and I'm afraid I've freaked him out. I know how skittish he can be sometimes. Just because he was so impatient for me today, doesn't mean he's there yet.

But he reassures me when he tips my head up with his fingers under my chin. "I...we're getting there. Aren't we?"

I don't press him for more because I know the truth. It's love he feels for me. It has to be, but maybe he's not ready to admit it just yet. I can wait.

Because I'm already there.

CHAPTER 25
NOAH

I don't think life has ever been more perfect.

Things with Jarred have been amazing. It seems like every day he's coming closer and closer to accepting himself, accepting us. It's a slow process, and sometimes I can see flashes of guilt in his eyes, but I don't blame him for that. After what he's been through in his life, I knew that this would be something that he'd struggle with for a long time. But he's trying. I can see the effort he's putting in when he's with me, every moment pushing himself just a little bit further and rejoicing at the little baby steps he takes.

Besides Jarred, camp has actually been pretty fucking fun. It's been nice seeing Ian blossom in these last two weeks, hanging out with more campers and putting himself out there. Kendall and Patrick are still great, including me in every plan they make even though I sometimes still just want to be by myself.

The only blip in this little peaceful bubble is the fact that it's Family Weekend at Camp Trinity. I'm not nervous about seeing my parents—counselors' parents aren't allowed in—but every other family member of the campers is invited to tour the camp for one day. I'm astonished at the amount of people that have shown up. It's like the first day of camp all over again but, still, that's not why I'm nervous.

"Why are you twitching?"

I look at Jarred where he stands beside me, handsome as ever in his Camp Trinity dress shirt, looking his best for the guests we're having today.

"I'm not twitching," I say stubbornly, even though I can feel the rhythmic tapping of my fingers against my leg.

"Yes, you are," he smiles. He cocks his head to the side and drops his voice to a whisper. "Baby, what's wrong?"

I lick my suddenly chapped lips. "Your kids are coming today."

"And?" His eyes widen slightly as he slips out a laugh at the realization he has. "Oh, you're nervous to meet my kids?"

"Well, yeah. I mean, I want them to like me," I say, fear thrumming in my chest. I know that his kids will have no idea who I am to their dad, but I still want their approval for myself. It doesn't help that it's awkward as fuck that they're six years older than I am. "What if they don't?"

"Our relationship isn't contingent on their approval," he states, and he risks twining his pinky with mine for a split second before pulling back. "But, if it makes you feel better, I think they'll love you."

I narrow my eyes at him. "You're lying to make me feel better."

"I'm not. Just be yourself, baby."

"Right," I say, taking in a deep breath. "I can do that."

I can be a slightly bitter, sometimes angry, sarcastic asshole, and they'll love that.

Crap, I'm screwed.

But something lightens in my chest because I know that's not what Jarred sees when he looks at me the way he's looking at me now. I almost want to tell him to school his features, but nobody is paying us any attention. When he looks at me this way—chocolate eyes filled with tenderness and love—I know he only sees the best of me. I feel like the best version of myself when I'm with him.

"Dad!"

My thoughts are interrupted as Jarred and I both look up to the source of the call.

Jesus fuck, his kids are *gorgeous*.

Two amazingly tall, brown-eyed, blond-haired supermodels approach us. His twins are smiling wildly as they run up to us, Mary immediately throwing herself in her dad's arms while Parker claps his back.

Jarred buries his nose in Mary's hair, rubbing her back before turning and hugging his son. "I'm so glad you two could make it this year."

I feel a bit awkward just standing here watching this interaction. Mary must notice because she cocks her head to the side with a welcoming smile as she looks at me. "Who's this?"

"This is Noah. Noah, this is Mary and Parker."

My chest puffs out a bit at the way he introduces me, his voice subtly laced with pride only I can hear. It gives me the confidence to give his twins a big wave and a wide smile. "Nice to meet you."

Jarred raises his brows because, yeah, maybe it's a little too much.

Mary looks puzzled for a moment before her smile returns. "Oh, well, nice to meet you."

"You too," I say, turning and shaking Parker's welcoming hand. "Jarred talks a lot about you."

"Really?" Parker asks, looking at Mary with an unreadable expression. "Well, it's nice to meet you."

"Dad, you're so sweet," Mary gushes, tossing her long blonde hair over her shoulder. She stiffens when she spots something behind us. "Oh no."

Parker's eyes widen. "Is that—"

"Mom."

We all turn around and my heart sinks when I see Jenny approaching us. I don't know why I thought she would look like a miserable hag, but I was one hundred percent wrong. She's...beautiful. Tall, just like Jarred and their kids, with poised features and startling white, blonde hair. She must be around Jarred's age but, just like him, she doesn't look it.

I'm hit with a stab of jealousy for a moment. A poisonous urge to stomp my feet like a child because she's *had* Jarred. I quickly push that away. No, Jarred chose *me*. I'm the one who's with him now. I'm the one that keeps him happy and satisfied, not this she-bitch that dared cheat on the most amazing man I've ever met.

"Jenny," Jarred says through gritted teeth, uncharacteristic anger in his voice as he greets her. "What are you doing here?"

Jenny looks startled but laughs it off. "It's Family Weekend. I'd never miss that."

"We're not a family anymore," Jarred spits out, and I want so much to reach for him and comfort him, but I know I can't. Thankfully, Mary does that for me, placing a delicate hand on her dad's shoulder.

"In the eyes of the Lord we are," Jenny states. She waves her hand dismissively, not even acknowledging her children. "I need to talk to you."

"I'm busy."

"You can spare a few minutes."

"No, he can't."

I bite my tongue two seconds too late. I should have just kept my mouth shut. All I've done is drawn Jenny's venomous eyes toward me, but can you blame me? Jarred was getting more agitated by the second. His frustration was seeping out of him painfully, and I couldn't have him be in pain. I was just defending him, but I've only managed to put my foot in my mouth.

"And who are you?" Jenny asks, narrowing her eyes at me, curling her lip in disgust as she looks me up and down.

"He's my…" Jarred clears his throat and doesn't look at me. "… camp counselor."

The reminder that we're not out together stings, but I brush it away. I understand why that was his answer. What is he going to say? *This is Noah, my nineteen-year-old lover? Oh, and by the way, I'm into guys?*

"It's none of your business what my husband and I need to discuss," she snaps, grabbing Jarred by the wrist. "Jarred. Come."

I think for a second he's going to fight against her, but I see his shoulders sag in defeat. If this is what it was like all their marriage, I can't imagine the frustration he must have felt for more than half of his life. Jenny is a vicious bitch and I want Jarred to tell her where to stick it, but his approach might be best to avoid a scene.

"Noah, why don't you take Mary and Parker around and show them this place hasn't changed much?" Jarred suggests, but I can read between the lines and see that it's more of a demand than a request.

It doesn't mean I have to like it.

"Fine," I grate, turning to Mary and Parker. "Let's go."

I hate the fact that my tone comes out clipped and annoyed, especially since I wanted to make a good first impression. Moody dick doesn't really seem to be something they'd like.

"So, Noah. What brought you to Camp Trinity?" Mary asks as she, Parker, and I make our way to the center of the camp. Her voice is airy and cheery, maybe trying to diffuse the tension I'm positive I'm carrying.

"You, know God and…stuff," I say, cringing at how lame that sounds.

"God…and stuff?" she repeats, a small little chuckle in her voice.

Parker snorts. "You're not really all about this, are you?"

They don't seem to be upset or scandalized by my apparent lack of interest, so I relax a bit, my lips tipping up in the corner. "What gave me away?"

"Are you liking it, though?" Parker asks as we pass by the chapel. "God and stuff aside?"

"Yeah, it's a really great place," I admit honestly, and I think of my favorite place to bring up. "I love the art studio."

Mary perks up. "Art was my favorite part of camp here. What kind do you do?"

"Acrylic based."

"I love that!"

I smile. Okay, so it isn't that hard to bond with his kids. "Do you want to see the studio?"

"Sure," Parker shrugs.

We head over to the art studio, and I head to the locked cabinet at the far end of the room once we're in. I start pulling out all of the work I've done so far—from a portrait of the sunset to an abstract rendition of a tree—and the twins enthusiastically look them over.

"Noah, these are gorgeous!" Mary gushes as Parker sifts through the rest of the paintings in the cabinet. "You're so talented!"

"What is this one?"

I don't move fast enough.

My eyes widen in horror as Parker pulls out the canvas I wasn't going to show them. I should have been more careful. I should have just stuck to the paintings the kids drew, but I wanted to impress Jarred's kids.

In Parker's hands and the focus of Mary's slack jaw is the painting I drew of Jarred and me in bed together.

"What...what is this?" Mary asks, her voice breathless and confused as she brings her finger down the canvas before looking up at me. "Noah?"

Parker shakes his head slowly. "Is this...Dad?"

I panic. "I can explain—"

"You're fucking our dad?" Parker asks, hands tightening around the canvas so hard I think he might tear it in half.

"No, I'm not," I lie quickly. "It's...it's just—"

"Oh, this is wonderful!"

"It's *what*?"

I stand before Parker and Mary, confused as fuck, and completely shocked when they both smile at each other with that creepy twin-like connection. They completely ignore me as they look at one another, another realization crossing through their identical faces. "This makes so much sense now."

Parker nods. "I know. I didn't think it would be this, though."

"Excuse me?" I interrupt, waving my hands in the air. "What the fuck is going on?"

Mary takes the canvas from Parker and sets it down on the table gently. "We know."

I furrow my eyebrows. "What do you mean, *you know*?"

"Well, we didn't know Dad was attracted to men, but we knew that he was dealing with something all his life. He was always so unhappy with Mom. So unhappy in general." She looks at her brother. "Today...Parker?"

Parker shakes his head with a chuckle. "You should have seen the way he looked at you when he introduced us, Noah. I've never seen him look at Mom that way before."

"So, you don't care that I'm a guy?" I ask, wondering when their eventual freakout will come. "You don't care that he's gay?"

Parker looks almost offended. "We're out in the real world. We're not as close-minded as you might think."

I blink back my shock. "Seriously?"

"Seriously," Mary says sweetly, grabbing my hand as she rubs her thumb against my palm. "All we ever wanted was for Dad to be happy. That's it. If you make him happy, we're happy."

"And you're okay that I'm younger than you are?" I chance, knowing that I'm probably pushing it.

Parker cringes. "Not going to lie, it's kind of weird."

I laugh that off. If anyone cares about my age, they can go fuck themselves. I can deal with Parker being weirded out by that, but I can't describe the amount of relief I feel that they're okay with this.

"He's going to be happy to hear that," I laugh, squeezing Mary's hand. "Well, after he gets embarrassed that you saw the painting."

"We should go and tell him," Mary says, turning to Parker. "He needs to know that we support him."

That's great and all but… "Maybe wait until there aren't hundreds of people he needs to entertain, and your mom isn't here."

"So smart," Mary coos, reaching over to ruffle my beanie-clad head. "Ugh, I can't wait to get to know you better."

"Since we have time, maybe you can show us around a bit more? Tell us about yourself?" Parker asks, something hopeful in his voice.

It's shitty the way they found out—Jarred should have been the one to tell him—but this eases a little bit of the tension in my chest.

Maybe this really can work out. If his kids are on board then maybe, it'll make the rest easier. Maybe it'll push him to finally live his true life.

Maybe everything is going to be okay.

CHAPTER 26
JARRED

"I don't like the way that young man spoke to me."

My jaw clenches and my face strains with the effort to remain impassive and relatively pleasant as I take Jenny away from the entrance of the camp. The last thing I need is to make a big scene, especially on such an important day as today.

"He probably didn't like your tone," I say, smiling and tipping my head at a passing parent.

"And all those piercings?" She gags, making the sign of the cross as she steps through the door and into the empty chapel I've led her to. "Ugh, what has this generation come to."

"Jenny, what the fuck are you doing here?" I snap and now that there's nobody around, I can let my anger show. "Seriously? What the fuck?"

"Watch how you speak to me, Jarred!" she hisses, narrowing her eyes at me. "I'm here because I'm your wife!"

I shake my head. "Soon-to-be ex-wife if you'd just sign those damn divorce papers already."

"Don't be ridiculous," she scoffs as she takes a seat in the back pew. She huffs as she pulls out her compact mirror from her purse, checking her reflecting and fussing over a stray hair coming out of her bun. "We're not getting a divorce. Why would you even say that?"

My jaw drops. "Excuse me?"

"Whether you like it or not, we're staying together," she puts plainly, smiling as if she isn't the wicked bitch she is.

"No, we're not."

"Well, I'm not signing the papers."

"Fuck, Jenny!" I shout at her stubbornness. She flinches, clutching at her imaginary pearls as she gapes at me.

"What's with the sudden language? You never used to be like this," she asks, her voice small as if I've actually struck her. That innocent act doesn't work on me. Not after two decades of marriage.

Weeks of marriage counseling, months of talking with lawyers, and years of feeling like I'm trapped have led to this. I can't make myself any clearer with her. I don't know what her insistence is on staying together, but there's no way in hell I'm letting her get away with talking me out of this. Not this time.

I've let her treat me like shit for more than half of my life. I've been her doormat, her servant, her figurative punching bag, and I can't take it anymore.

"Because you never let me! You controlled everything about my life, and I just took it! I'm tired of that! I have someone now that appreciates who I am and doesn't treat me like shit!"

Her eyes widen as her compact mirror drops to the floor. "You're… you're with someone?"

I bypass her shock that someone could possibly want me and nod. "Yes."

"Who?" she barks, standing and marching up to me with venom in her eyes. "Who could possibly be worth ending our marriage?"

"Noah!"

His name slips off my lips before I have the chance to think better of it. It's the automatic reaction I didn't know I had. Fear strikes me. The plan hadn't been to say anything about Noah but now that it's out there, it's out there.

Jenny looks as shocked as I feel but confused all the same like she didn't quite hear me right. "What did you say?"

"It's Noah. Jenny…" I take a deep breath, my clenched fists trembling at my side. "I'm gay."

And then it hits me. That clarity I was searching for. That certainty I craved when I spoke to Father Matteo. That feeling of joyous relief finally hits me. It's terrifying, exhilarating, but ultimately…freeing.

I said it.

I'm gay.

I'm gay and in love with Noah Scott.

I said it and God hasn't smitten me. I said it and the world is still turning. I said it and I'm still alive and breathing. I said it and it felt so *fucking* good.

"I'm a gay man," I repeat, clearer and louder this time, a smile threatening to split my face. "I'm a gay man and I'm in love with Noah."

"N—No, no you're not," Jenny stutters, shaking her head as she takes a step back. "That's ridiculous! That terrible boy has corrupted you!"

"You watch your fucking mouth when you talk about him!" I snap, pointing a dangerous finger at her. "Deal with it. I love Noah, and I'd choose him over you any day."

She snarls at me, swatting my hand down as she shoves my chest. "How dare you turn your back on God!"

Am I really turning my back on God? Am I willing to sacrifice everything I've ever known, everything I've ever believed, for a man who might not love me back?

The answer is yes. In the choice between God and Noah, I choose Noah. In the choice between a life of misery and happiness, I choose happiness.

"At least I'm not a cheater," I say with a breathless laugh. "I'm finally happy for once in my life. You gave me the twins, Jenny. I'll always be thankful for that, but you have no place in my world anymore."

"Of course, I don't," she growls, gathering her belongings with haste and violence. "Mark my words, God is going to punish you for this. God will see to it that you are made an example of for every person out there with deviant thoughts like yours."

I take her words in, but they don't have the effect she wanted. God won't punish me. There's nothing God could do to me that I can't face with Noah by my side. I don't know what this means for the camp, but I do know that Jenny won't breathe a word of this. She wouldn't be able to cope with people knowing that she was married to a gay man for twenty-five years. It would humiliate her.

My secret is still safe. I'll get it all. Noah and the camp.

I leave her, stunned in the chapel, and head toward the dining hall. Fighting with her has taken up too much of my time, and it's about the hour that the highlight reel is going to start. I'm still trembling from leftover adrenaline, but I walk with a purpose. I make sure that my steps are confident as I enter the dining hall, seeing that Kendall and Patrick have already set up the big screen and the projector.

Every year, we do a highlight reel for Family Weekend, just to show off what the kids have spent the summer doing and what they'll continue to do in the two weeks left of camp. It's nothing super fancy, and only parents are allowed in, while the rest of the campers prepare a special presentation by the lake.

"Everything okay, Mr. Walker?" Kendall asks me when I reach her. She cocks her head to the side and scowls. "I'm sorry, but you seem...flustered."

I beam at her. Flustered is the right word. I just dropped a major bomb and haven't had proper time to think it through, but I know everything will be okay. "It's Jarred, Kendall. Yes, it is. Is everything ready?"

"Yes, sir," Patrick confirms, reading through the clipboard in his hands. "Bryce brought the film by earlier. We're still missing a few parents, but I'm sure they'll filter in soon. We were just waiting for you to start."

I look around for Noah and see that he isn't here with us. I would have liked him to see the highlight reel. Unknowingly, or by pure instinct, he's in a lot of the footage. I'm not upset, though because this means things must be going well with him and the twins.

I nod quickly, walking up in front of the projector, ready to greet the parents. As usual, I feel a tingle of nerves whenever I speak in front of a large crowd, but I push it down. I'm proud of what I've accomplished this summer, and I'm confident enough to admit that I want to show it off. "Hello, parents and guardians! I want to welcome you to Camp Trinity! How is everybody doing today?"

There's a resounding cheer that echoes through the dining hall. I let their energy fuel me, feeling higher than ever. "Amazing! As you might know, these last couple of months have been great. I'm sure that your children have grown to appreciate God and all his wonders during their time here. The goal of Camp Trinity has always been to help them on their journey to become bright young individuals who approach the world with kindness and compassion. As per tradition, we've made a highlight reel of our time here at camp! I hope you enjoy it!"

Another round of claps fills the room as I take a step back, standing tall and proud next to the projector. My chest swells with affection for all the kids as the video plays—images of them showing off their new skills, clips of them making new friends, snippets of the happiest moments of their lives—and I'm reminded again of why I do this.

But then…

No.

Oh no.

How is it that your world can shatter in just a split second? There's that split second—that one moment—when you know that everything is about to crash down around you.

It's that feeling of landing on the concrete after free falling, your guts splattered on the ground, your blood pooling out of your mouth, your shit coming out of your ass. Lifeless and reduced to nothing.

And that's how I feel right now, watching Noah fuck me on the big screen.

"What…" My heart seizes and all the blood rushes to my cheeks. I don't know what to say. I don't know what to do. I don't know how this could have happened.

How the fuck did this happen?

Kendall gasps beside me, transfixed by the image on the screen, tears springing in her eyes. "Mr. Walker, what is this?"

"I…" But I don't have any words. I recognize what's playing on the screen. It was one of the times when Noah and I snuck over to my cabin in the middle of the day to fuck. I had no idea someone had noticed us. I had no idea anybody would *film* it. "No. No. No…"

"You should be arrested!"

"This is a disgrace!"

"Why would you show this to us!"

"I can't believe I sent my *children* here!"

"Pervert!"

I'm assaulted all at once as I back away from the screen as the once-happy parents turn into a righteous mob. I don't blame them. This *is* sick and twisted. This *is* perverted.

That beautiful moment with Noah has been tainted and broadcasted for everyone to see, and I can only stand like an idiot as I watch my world collapse all around me. So, I do the only thing I can think of.

I run.

The reel still plays in the background as I run into a broad body. I'm ready to fight the parent off me in my attempt to escape, but the smell of cigarette smoke fills my lungs and I realize it's not one of them.

Noah looks panicked as he stops me right outside the dining hall. His hands automatically reach for my cheeks, his eyes wide with concern. "Jarred, what's wrong? Why are you—"

He stops in his tracks, however, when he hears his obscene command that I come filter through the open door. He looks just as shocked as I feel but steels himself with a determined resolve in those hazel eyes.

Not letting go of me, he barks into the room. "Turn that shit off! Babe, it's okay—"

"This can't be happening!" I screech, pushing his hands away from me. They feel like blood and poison, diseased and sickly.

"It's okay," Noah coos, casting a nervous glance behind me. "It's all going to be okay."

"Get the fuck off me!" I growl, ripping myself out of his open arms because it's not going to be okay. Nothing is ever going to be okay again.

I run as fast as my feet can carry me, ignoring when the parents try to stop me with their hateful words and disgusted looks. They have every right to be angry. They have every right to hate me.

Almost as much as I hate myself.

I did this. I brought this upon myself. By choosing Noah over God, by not being able to resist temptation, and by allowing myself to indulge in carnal sin, I've turned God against me.

God is punishing me and sending me straight to hell.

And it's all Noah's fault.

CHAPTER 27
NOAH

"Who the fuck did this?" I yell, rage coursing through my veins, the monster inside me coming to the surface. The sounds of Jarred and me play through the room, but I ignore it when I catch a smug face staring at me. "*You!*"

I barrel my way to Bryce, knocking him on his ass as I grip his collar. I raise and bang his body against the floor, seething with so much anger I think I might burst.

"What?" Bryce chuckles, eyes flickering to the screen where my sex tape still plays. "You didn't like the show?"

I can't help myself. I think of Jarred's panicked face. I think of what this is going to mean. I think of everything besides a rational thought as my fist lands and cracks against Bryce's nose. "You fucking asshole! Why did you do that?"

"Because Jarred shouldn't be running this camp! Because what you two are is a disgrace to everything this camp stands for!" he yells, spitting up some blood that's trickled down to his lips. "I couldn't just let this go by and accept that a man like him was trying to teach children about God!"

"No, you sick son of a bitch! You did this for your own amusement! What if there had been kids in the audience? I'm going to kill you!"

Before I can strike him again, small hands are trying to pry me away from this fucking lunatic with a death wish. I fight against it, my ears ringing and my vision going hazy. I want Bryce's blood. I want his pleas to stop. I want his cries. They're going to fucking nourish me for the rest of my life.

"Noah!" Kendall screams, still trying to get me up. "No!"

I struggle, fighting against her iron grip on my wrist as I go for Bryce again. "Let go of me!"

"No, you're going to do something you regret!"

"Trust me, I won't regret it!"

"Patrick, help me!"

Once there are two bodies pulling at me, my own strength weakens. I'm dragged away from that piece of shit Bryce, hauled across the room, and thrown into the kitchen. I still see red. The sex tape is still playing, mocking me for not fucking Bryce up more than I did. I rush to the kitchen doors, but Kendall blocks my path.

"Let me out!" I roar, not wanting to hit her, but needing to get out there and torture that fucker.

She places her hands on my chest to push me back. "No!"

"Noah, calm down," Patrick begs, coming up behind me to wrap his arms around my chest. He's not trying to hold me back. He's almost hugging me. "Breathe with me, Noah. Think about Jarred."

Jarred. The man of my literal dreams. The one whose livelihood was just destroyed. The look on his face when he ran out of the dining hall, it was excruciating. It looked like someone had stabbed a knife into his stomach and dragged it painfully up to his chest. I don't know if he realized he had been crying, but thick fat tears were streaming down his face.

I feel like a complete failure because I promised I'd keep him safe. I told myself I'd protect Jarred from anything. I made a vow that Bryce would never do anything to harm us. Although I never could have predicted this, I failed him.

"I can't believe Bryce did that," I sob, letting Patrick's embrace pry out the agony of what just happened. "I...I need to see Jarred."

"What Jarred might need is some space," Kendall says with a sympathetic shake of her head. "You saw what just happened."

I shake my own head. "You don't know that. You don't know him like I do."

"Kendall's right," Patrick says, letting go of me when he realizes I'm not going to run. "He just had your sex tape flashed on the screen in front of the parents of every kid here. Give him a minute."

"I should have known. You've been sneaking out every night, I just thought you were out for a smoke," Kendall says, coming up to me and hugging me. "Oh, Noah. I'm so sorry this happened."

"Bryce is going to die."

"No, he's not," she says sternly, grabbing my face roughly. "We're going to get the police involved like rational adults, but first, we need to deal with this."

"How are we going to deal with this?" Patrick questions, eyes wide as he bites the corner of his lip. "I...I don't know what we can do."

Kendall huffs and takes a step back. She paces in front of us with her fingers resting on her temple until she snaps them in the air. "Let's give the parents a second to cool off. Once they do, I'll go out there and explain the situation. Jarred didn't know that was going to happen. I'll make them understand."

"I don't think they will," I whisper, dropping my face into my hands. "This is too much for anybody to understand."

The doors to the kitchen fly open as Mary and Parker come tumbling in. Mary immediately races up to me, almost knocking me over as she wraps me in her arms. "Oh my God!"

"Mary," I choke out, clinging to her with remorse. "I'm so sorry—"

"What?" she questions, baffled when she pulls back. "It's not your fault! Obviously, that was filmed without your consent. *You* have nothing to apologize for."

"I turned that shit off," Parker spits, shaking his head with disgust. "Nobody needs to see what you and my dad have. It's none of their fucking business."

"Have you seen him?" I question desperately. "Where is he?"

"He was running to the cabin the last time I saw him."

I rip myself away from her. "I need to see him."

Jarred's panicking. He's going to have a panic attack. He's going to feel so alone, so humiliated, so betrayed, and I need to be there for him. I promised him I'd be there no matter what, and this is that exact situation. He needs to know that he'll have me through anything that could hit us.

Kendall shakes her head. "He needs his space—"

"No! I have to see him!"

I shove past them before they can stop me, and they do try. I ignore the looks from the parents who are obviously putting two and two together and coming up with the fact that I was the one in the video with Jarred. I couldn't care less what they think. The man I love is all I care about.

There are some parents already outside, ushering their kids to the cars. It's chaos and frenzy, but I don't care.

Jarred. Jarred. Jarred.

I reach his cabin and nearly face-plant against the door when I realize it's locked. "Jarred!" I cry as I bang on the door. "Jarred! It's me! Let me in!"

I have to knock ferociously on the door a couple more times and stumble when it swings open. Jarred is the first thing I see but then I notice the mess surrounding us. He's ripped up the entire cabin. All the artwork on the walls is scattered on the ground. The sheets are torn in half like he did it with his own bare hands. Dishes are broken, knick-knacks are destroyed, and I have to believe it looks exactly like how Jarred feels.

"Jarred, babe, holy shit," I say, wanting nothing more than to pull him into my arms. I take his trembling hands in my own as I pull him toward me. "It's going to be okay. Trust me. We'll get through this."

"No."

"What?"

I pull away from him and he takes a step back. He distances himself like a wounded animal would from a vicious predator. His face is nothing like I've seen before. All that anger and all that shame has made him into somebody I don't recognize. "Don't you see what this is? God is punishing us."

"No, he's not," I argue, scoffing with exasperation because fucking *God* had nothing to do with this. "It was Bryce. For whatever reason, he did this."

"*God* did this," Jarred says, pulling at his hair as he kicks over his dining room chair. "I knew what we were doing was wrong, and I didn't seek forgiveness."

I throw my hands up in the air, begging him to see reason. "Because there's nothing to forgive! Babe, God had nothing to do with this! We need to deal with the situation!"

"No. What you need to do is leave."

"Fuck that. I'm not going anywhere."

"Yes, you are! I don't want you anymore!" he roars, narrowing his eyes at me like I'm some sort of evil supervillain. "Don't you see? This was all a big mistake! Everything I've ever worked for has been ruined because of *you*!"

My heart stops as I feel all the blood drain from my face. "You... you don't mean that."

"You've corrupted me! Sullied me! Damned me to hell!"

"You don't mean that either." I take a deep breath and try to calm my twisting stomach. Jarred is just shocked. He's just been through a traumatic event. He has so much anger and he's taking it out on me. "Babe, what we have is beautiful. What we have is—"

"Is disgusting!" he shouts, throwing a glass against the wall where it shatters with a crunching groan. "You were a manipulative demon that was sent to test me, and I failed! It's an abomination! *You*, Noah, are an abomination!"

I step back as if he's punched me. His words slice through my heart. They shatter me just like the glass against the wall. This isn't happening. Just this morning, we were happy. We were happy and in love and meeting his kids and working toward a future.

And Bryce has ruined that all.

"I love you, Jarred. Please, don't do this to us," I plead, going against my better judgment and hugging him. "Please. Please, see that."

He pushes me away from him so hard that I nearly fall to the ground. When he looks down at me, all I see is hatred. It's not the kind of repulsion that can be faked. He truly believes I did this to him. He truly believes everything he's said. His fists are clenched, his upper lip is curled in a snarl, and those once beautiful eyes are dark with vengeance.

He turns his back on me. "I'll be praying for you, Noah."

"Jarred—"

"*Leave!*"

And I do because I can't take another second of this. I leave his cabin, tears streaming down my face, snot pouring out of my nose, and my heart breaking over and over again at his words.

Because Jarred chose God over me.

CHAPTER 28
JARRED

Over half of the campers have left. I've been told that the camp is a ghost of what it used to be. Not that I know. I haven't left my cabin in a week.

Father Matteo has stopped by. He told me he tried to explain to the parents what happened, but the damage had already been done. Everything that I've worked for my entire life is gone. Camp Trinity is over.

Mary told me Bryce was the one behind the tape, that Kendall confirmed it when she and Patrick cornered him, but I don't know what happened with him. I don't care.

I've been broken. Beaten. Buried.

I'm done.

"Dad?"

I look over at Mary who's holding a steaming cup of coffee in her hand. "Maybe you should have some coffee?"

I take another swig of the vodka I had stored from a long time ago when I tried using alcohol to drown the demons out. "I don't want to talk, Mary."

"You haven't come out of here since…" Parker doesn't finish his sentence. "Dad, this isn't healthy."

They should go home. They've put their lives on hold for me, and they shouldn't. Mary and Parker told me that they knew about Noah before the video. They've told me that they're okay with it, that they encourage my happiness, that God had nothing to do with what happened, but I'm not sure I believe them.

I'm a rotten soul. Not only for what I did to this camp but for what I did to Noah.

Beautiful, perfect Noah. He's gone. Mary confirmed that when I broke two days ago and asked about him. I regret everything that happened between us—not the love, not the sex, not the joy—but the things I said to him, the way I acted, and the things I made him believe.

The things I said to him...

I deserve to be punished for that too.

I look up just as Father Matteo walks into the cabin. He's been a frequent visitor, but I haven't wanted to talk to him either. He looks at the bottle in my hand and sighs before turning to the twins. "Mary, Parker. Why don't you help Kendall and Patrick and make sure the campers are settled for dinner?"

Mary and Parker share a look but nod. Mary kisses my cheek as Parker squeezes my shoulder before they exit, leaving me alone with Father Matteo.

"What are you doing here, Father?" I ask him, my words slurring as I take another swig of the vodka.

"We're all worried about you, Jarred," Father Matteo says, sitting down on the bed next to me. "I thought that maybe you're ready to talk."

"What is there to talk about?" I laugh cruelly. "I sinned. I laid with another man, and this is what happened. I wish I had never met Noah."

Father Matteo frowns. "Do you really mean that, Jarred?"

No, I don't. That's the part that's so painstakingly difficult. I don't believe it and I don't mean it. Ever since I forced Noah out that door, I've wanted him back. But I don't know what to do. I don't know how to reconcile these parts of myself—the parts that crave him and the parts that know it's wrong—and it's driving me insane.

How can I want what I know I can't have? Why does it feel like someone ripped out my heart when I think about Noah? When I think about God, why do I feel like being without Noah is the punishment I deserve?

It's all a confusing mess, and I don't know how to sort through it all. So, I drink. I drink and I sleep and I let myself fall deeper and deeper into despair because I did this to myself.

"Your kids love you, Jarred. There are parents here who still support you. The world is a different place now," Father Matteo says, taking the bottle gently out of my hands. "Why don't you try reaching out to Noah?"

"How can you say that?" I ask, agonized that he would even bring him up. "What about God—"

"Enough bullshit about God!"

I gasp. In the ten years I've known him, Father Matteo has *never* raised his voice like that. Not only that, but he's a priest. His words strike me to my core, and I'm left only to gape at him. "Father Matteo—"

"No, you listen to me," he snaps, brows furrowed and eyes narrowed as he slams the bottle down on my nightstand. "Fuck all that! Fuck it all! Do you love Noah?"

More than anything. More than God. More than myself.

But how is that okay? Why is the guilt still eating me alive? Why does it have to be a choice?

"Yes," I whisper, wishing that it was Noah here to comfort me, to scream at me, to just do *anything* to me. "But—"

"No buts," he interrupts. "God is fucking love, Jarred. That's all he is. He doesn't give a shit if you're straight or gay. God is who you want him to be."

"That can't be true," I say, desperation seeping through my voice. "That's not what I've spent my life believing."

"Because you've been brainwashed. You've been told that there was something so innately wrong with you, but we're still here. God is still here." Father Matteo sighs, pinching the bridge of his nose as he takes his own swig of the vodka. He thinks for a moment, teetering with the bottle in his hand before turning back to me. "When do you feel closest to God?"

I know what my answer should be. I should say that I feel closest to God when I attend mass. I should say I feel his presence when I pray. I should say that I believe in him the most when I take in His holy spirit, but I don't.

If God is all the wonders of the world, all the majesty of the universe, and all the goodness in the cosmos, I only feel that with one person.

"When I'm with Noah," I answer, my voice small and frail. I feel tears well in my eyes as I drop my face into my hands. "Father, I'm so confused. I don't want to feel this guilt anymore. I don't want to feel this shame. I just want Noah."

"And there's nothing wrong with that," he assures me, rubbing my back in soothing circles. "When we had our talk about Noah, you were so close to acceptance. Don't let the act of a cowardly little shit change that. If you love Noah, you should be with him."

I shake my head as I wipe away the snot on my nose. "I don't think I can. I'm ashamed of the things I've said to him. He'd never take me back after that."

"You need to try," he insists. He pries my hands away from my face and smiles gently. "Forget about everything else. You can deal with all the things you feel once you have him by your side. Take this day by day, Jarred, but don't deny yourself the happiness you deserve."

I don't know if I deserve it, but I want it. I still don't know what exactly I feel, but I do know that I love Noah. Father Matteo is right. If I take this day by day, I know I'll find the answer. But I can't do that when I'm living with the other half of my soul, ripped away and torn to shreds inside my barely beating heart.

Father Matteo hands me a piece of paper with an address scrawled in neat handwriting on the top. "I had Kendall text him and ask him where he was. He's back home with his parents. His address was on file."

"Can you watch the camp while I'm gone?" I ask.

He nods, giving me a reassuring grin. "Go to him, Jarred. God will guide you to the right choice. I know it seems hopeless, but He will be with you—always."

I hold onto the paper like it's a lifeline. I have a choice to make now.

Do I let the best thing that's ever happened to me slip away because of my own cowardice? Do I bend to the will of my dead father's wishes? Do I...do I choose God?

But it's not a choice, is it? If what Father Matteo said is true, then I can have both. I can have Noah and still believe in God. I don't know how, but I can. I have to believe that there's an answer to this fucked-up puzzle I'm just missing.

But I know I can't do it without Noah.

CHAPTER 29
NOAH

I toss another handful of popcorn at the screen. Why did I choose to watch this again? Two sexy exorcists trying to save the soul of a single father is so not what I should be watching right now. I'm just torturing myself with this glaring reminder of *God*.

A god who—if he exists—has royally screwed me over.

I don't even realize I'm crying until I taste tears on my lips. I'm lucky my parents aren't around to witness this because I don't know what I'd say. Thankfully, they haven't asked about why I left camp so early. All they know is that there was a sex tape leaked, but they don't know it was me in the video with Jarred.

Jarred.

The tears fall even quicker, just like they do every time I think of him.

I never imagined I could feel this type of pain. I thought that my parents not truly loving me was the worst I could feel but that's a dull ache compared to what Jarred did. His words replay like an infinite loop in my brain. The things he called me are sticky reminders of my worth.

Abomination.

Maybe that is what I am. Maybe that's all I'm meant to be. A poisonous, manipulative asshole who brings everyone down. I ruined my parents' life by not being the perfect son. I ruined Jarred's life by destroying his camp. I ruin what I touch.

I stopped believing in God years ago but if He really is out there, He must hate me too.

I devolve in a fit of tears. Angry, thick, desperate tears that don't seem to end. I've cried every day this week, and I thought at some point it would have to end. Only a knock on the door puts me out of my misery. I try my best to make it look like I wasn't just having a meltdown as I wrap my fluffy blanket around my shoulders and answer the door but what greets me makes the tears come back up to the surface.

"J—Jarred? What are you doing here?"

I never expected to see Jarred again. While my stomach is doing happy little backflips at seeing him, my mind roars against it. It doesn't help that he looks exactly like I feel—battered and broken. His jaw is filled with scruff that wasn't there before and deep bags hang under his eyes. Like mine probably are, his eyes are rimmed-red, puffy, and swollen. He's never looked more like his true age than he does now.

"Can I come in?" His voice is cracked and weak, his lips chapped and matching the color of his pale skin. "Noah?"

"I..." I hold back the part of me that wants to throw myself at him. "I think it's best if we talk out here."

He nods, and I don't know what to say. I don't know what to do. He made it exceedingly clear the last time I saw him that he wanted nothing to do with me anymore. Nothing rivaled his brutality when he cast me away. Even now, looking at his lips, the reminder stings. His lips weren't meant to spill those kinds of cruel words, not when he made me promise I'd be his no matter what.

Betrayal cracks at my heart and all that anger I try to keep at bay resurfaces.

"What are you doing here? How do you know where I live?" I snap, pulling the blanket tighter around me as if it'll act as some sort of shield.

"Kendall told me."

I bite back a curse. I knew I shouldn't have said a thing. Kendall's great, but she has a big heart. She mentioned before I left that Jarred just needed more time, but I didn't have more time to give. My heart could only take so much suffering.

"Noah, I'm so sorry," he says, eyes watering as he tries to give me a shaky smile, his lips trembling with the effort. "It's so good to see you, baby."

"You can't say that to me," I bite, taking a step away from him. "Not after what you did to me."

He hangs his head in what I can only assume is shame. "I know what I did was wrong. Everything I said, I was wrong. You're none of the things I called you, Noah. I need you to know that."

"You ripped me apart," I cry, not being able to hold back my agony. "Was I worth nothing to you?"

His head snaps back up and his pleading brown eyes pierce through me. "You're everything to me. You saved me from myself, and you made me realize that I'm worthy of the love I choose. I choose you, baby. Over God, I choose you."

I sob. One broken, tragic sob because he's learned nothing. Because maybe if he had said something else, this would be okay. If he had said anything else, I would jump into his arms because I want him now just as badly as I did a week ago.

But he's learned nothing. He's accepted nothing. He's forgiven nothing.

"It shouldn't be a choice," I choke out with a shake of my head. "Don't you get that?"

"I love you. This is…this is all I have."

"It's not good enough."

We're both crying now—openly and savagely—because we know what we had is in the wind. It's left behind in the dusk of the day, a forgotten secret we should have known was too good to be true.

What he's offering simply isn't good enough. I can see that he still carries shame and guilt, and I don't blame him. If I was taught all my life that who I was would send me to hell, I'd be the same way too. If I had a father who abused and tortured me for loving men, I wouldn't be able to accept it either.

But I can't go back to him now, not when there's a chance that he'll break and break me again in the process.

"I'll do anything," he begs, reaching out to grab my hands, and my traitorous body doesn't pull away. *"Anything,* Noah. I'll leave the church. I'll shut down the camp. I'll move next to UNC. I'll do anything to be with you again."

I grit my teeth and tremble. "It's *not good enough."*

And before I can stop him, he's kissing me. It's tormenting me with all the pleasure I thought I'd never have again. It's reminding me of how much I love him, how much I crave him, how much I'd give for him. It almost breaks my resolve—the way his lips bruise mine with such passion—but I resist.

"No," I growl as I rip myself away, his lips chasing after me. "I love you, Jarred, but I love me too. You're not ready to love me the way I deserve to be loved. You still think that it's me versus God, and it's not. Until that changes, you can't be a part of my life."

"Baby, please—"

"No," I say, firmer this time as I white knuckle the edge of the door. "You need to go."

He wants to argue with me. I can see it in his eyes. He wants to fight for us, but there's nothing for us to fight for yet. He wants me to fight for us, but I've fought as much as I could.

I close the door on his face, not hearing his final plea as I lean against the frame and drop to the floor. I let out a wail, a moan, an ear-piercing scream because I want him too.

But I have to learn to love myself again before I can love him.

CHAPTER 30
NOAH

In the next two weeks, it's been nothing but texts from Jarred and calls that I ignored every night. He's persistent in his attempts to tell me he's changed. He's ruthless in his quest to make me see that we belong together. That's the fucked-up thing. I know we do, but no number of words will change the fact that he's just not ready.

I'm sitting at breakfast with my parents, swirling around the grits in front of me. I don't really want to eat. I haven't been hungry in a long time. Even when I do it, it tastes like nothing. Bland. Lifeless. Just like me, I guess.

Every time Jarred reaches out, I want to answer. I need him back in my life. I almost cave when I replay his declaration of love. But then I remember that he called me an abomination, that something deep inside him still believes that, and I don't.

I didn't realize loving someone was supposed to hurt this much.

"Noah," my mother says, patting at her black bun as she gestures at my plate. "You better finish. We're going to be late for church."

I push around the grits and shake my head. Their continued attempts to get me to go to church have failed in the last two weeks. I don't know why they think it'll work this Sunday. "I'm not going."

My father huffs with a scowl. "Your mother and I let it slide the last two Sundays because you've been a wreck, but you have to go to church. Out of all the time in your week, why can't you give God two hours of it?"

"Is it because of that man?" my mother asks, tipping her head to the side as she frowns. "Are you still traumatized by what happened at camp?"

They still don't know it was me in that video. They haven't even brought it up since they heard it through the grapevine that first day I came back. I don't think they'd be as accepting of my behavior if they knew it was me fucking Jarred. I've let them believe that because I don't want to talk about it. I don't see the point in admitting it. It wouldn't change a thing.

It wouldn't erase the heartbreak or rewind the clock.

My father sighs, pushing his thick glasses up his nose. "This is our fault."

My head snaps up as I furrow my brows at him. "What do you mean?"

"We thought that camp would help you come to your senses about this new lifestyle of yours, but we didn't realize that pervert would only make it worse."

"He...he's not a pervert," I mumble because my first instinct is to come to his defense. "He's gay. So, what?"

"What do you mean? We trusted that man to take care of you," my mother snaps, throwing her hands up in the air. "All this time, he's only been a deviant. We're lucky that you didn't come back as tainted as he is."

"He's not tainted," I say through gritted teeth. "He's actually pretty great."

"You don't have to defend the man," my father says. "People like you don't deserve that. I swear, out of all the sick people in this world, we had to send you to a camp that had someone like him."

The word has never stung before, but it does now. Jarred isn't sick and he isn't a deviant and he isn't a pervert. Despite the things he said to me, he's wonderful. He's a wonderful human being who doesn't know what he wants. This doesn't make him a bad person. This doesn't make him a leper.

My mother's hand flies over her heart. "To think of what thoughts he could have poisoned those children with—"

And that makes me crack. The mere implication that Jarred would ever do anything to harm one of his campers get<u>s</u> to me. He's dedicated his entire life to helping children grow and learn. He's prided himself on his camp, which only ever brought people joy. He doesn't deserve to be vilified.

I become angry once again. My natural defenses rise along with my hackles. I'll still protect Jarred from anybody who dares harm him, even if he's not present to hear it himself. I just love him that much.

"Enough!" I yell, slamming my hands on the table as I stand. "He didn't do anything to the children! He didn't do anything wrong!"

"How can you say that?"

"Because I was the one in the video with him!"

They both gasp in outrage. Their faces contort in a mixture of disbelief and revulsion. It looks like my father can't quite believe it, but my mother turns on me in an instant. "So, *you're* responsible for ruining that man's life?"

"Yeah," I gulp. "I am."

"Of course, it all comes back to you. Why do you insist on rebelling every chance you get? Why can't you let God—"

"Holy fucking shit! Enough of God!" I shout because I can't hear any more about Him. God's been enough of a presence in my life for the last three months and I can't fucking take it anymore. "I hate God!"

My father slams his hands on the table. "Noah Scott!"

"If you're really as sick as you're saying, you need to leave!"

I gape at my mother. "What?"

"You heard your mother! We did not raise you to be like this! We did not raise you to forsake God like this!" my father bellows, standing up to pull me roughly to my feet. "If you're going to live in sin, you're not going to do it under our roof!"

I've always known they never approved of me, but this still comes as a shock. I knew they threatened to stop paying for my college, but I never considered that they would kick me out.

But I realize slowly that I'm...*relieved*. If I really want to change, if I want to be better, if I want to move on with my life, I have to love myself. I have to put myself first. I have to realize that I'm worth more.

You're everything to me.

And with his voice in my mind, I rip my arm away from my father. "Fucking gladly!"

I storm out of the kitchen and out of the house, away from all the hate I grew up with and with the promise of a brighter future without those leeches dragging me down. I might be a bit terrified that I don't have a place to live and that I definitely don't have a way to pay for school, but everything will be okay.

Because I chose me first.

My phone rings, and I pull it out of my pocket and answer it without looking. "Hello?"

"Noah? Christ, thank you for answering."

I wish I had looked at the caller ID. This is the last thing I need right now. "Jarred. Goodbye—"

"Baby! Don't hang up!"

I go to do just that, but his voice is so desperate. I can admit that it's so good to hear it after this time apart. It soothes the anxiety, bringing me a kind of peace I don't know I realized I was missing. Something in me softens, and I sigh into the receiver, unconsciously clutching it tighter against my cheek as I sit down on the sidewalk in front of my house. "Fine. What do you want to say?"

"I was wondering if you'd consider coming back to Camp Trinity."

I scoff. "Camp is over."

"No, I know. I just..." He trails off and I can hear him sniffle on the other side of the line. *"I've made some changes I want you to see."*

"My parents kicked me out," I say, not too sure why I'm telling him this.

He gasps on the other end. *"What? Are you okay?"*

Yeah? I guess. I'm sure it'll hit me later that I'm practically homeless, but I don't want to talk about that now.

"Noah?"

I can hear the genuine concern in his voice, and I crack. I take a deep breath before nodding. "I'll come back if only because I need a place to crash until I figure my shit out."

"I'll take it," he says, and his enthusiasm and relief are apparent.

"I'll be there in a few hours," I say, knowing I have to wait until my parents go to church to sneak back inside and get my shit. I hang up without saying anything else.

I'm going to see Jarred again, but my will is strong. I won't take him back unless he's changed. I'll resist the urge to beg him to kiss me and choose me and love me.

I just hope I'm not making a mistake that'll shatter the already tattered pieces of my soul.

CHAPTER 31
JARRED

I think the last time I felt this nervous was when the twins were born.

I'm standing at the entrance of the camp, smoothening down the wrinkles of my button-down shirt before scraping my nails against my smooth jaw. I wanted to look nice for Noah. I know it's only been a couple of weeks, but it's felt like forever since I've seen him.

I've called him every day during our time apart, but he hadn't answered the phone until today. Something pleasant and hopeful bubbles in my stomach. He's really coming here. I'm going to get to see him. I'll get the chance to finally win him back, to prove that he can count on me now. I know it's going to take everything I have to convince him that I didn't mean the horrible things I said to him, but I need to try. If there's even a chance that he'll take me back, I need to give it my all.

My heart seizes when I see him coming up the camp entrance. I clear my throat and plaster a smile on my face, waving at him like an idiot as he approaches me. I almost frown because he looks just like he did when he first entered the camp—angry and bitter—but with an underlying sadness to him that wasn't there before.

"Noah," I breathe, licking my chapped lips as I take him in. "I'm so happy you're here."

"I didn't really have anywhere else to go," he says with a shrug after taking a long drag of his cigarette. "It was this or my car."

I try not to let the comment sting. "But you're here."

"Yeah, but I'm here," he says slowly with a heavy sigh, hazel eyes meeting mine under his lashes. He purses his lips as he looks away from me. "So, I guess I can stay in my old bunk?"

My cheeks flush. Was I an idiot to assume that he would stay with me? Yes, I was. It's practically a miracle that he agreed to come in the first place. I nod. "Um, yeah. If you want."

"I do," he says quickly, rushing through his words as if they pain him. He steels himself with resolution as he looks me dead in the eyes. "You said you wanted to show me something?"

"Yeah," I say. "Go for a walk? We're actually coming back the way you came."

"Fine," he says, putting out his cigarette under his booted foot.

The hope in my chest dims. Maybe there really is no getting him back. Regardless, I'm going to persist. There is no other option than bringing him back to me. He's everything I care about, everything I want, and I know that we belong together. He's still carrying his duffel bag as we make our way down the trail to the parking lot of the camp. I take him to where the camp sign is, proudly displayed just where the woods thin into a scattered clearing.

"So, Camp Trinity is officially closed," I say, fingering the tarp over the camp sign.

His eyes widen and he nearly drops his duffle. "What? They can't do that."

"No, Noah. I did it."

"Why?"

I play with the tarp, chewing on the inside of my cheek. "Because although I loved Camp Trinity, it doesn't stand for what I believe anymore. Want to see the name of the new camp?"

He nods, and I take a deep breath before pulling the tarp off the sign. I haven't actually seen the new sign either, wanting to wait for Noah to be here so we can do it together. When I take it in, it's life-changing. Carved in a meticulous script, the color of a rainbow is—

Camp Acceptance.

Noah sucks in a sharp breath before his fingers brush over the wooden sign, transfixed and with a small smile on his face. "It's a nice name."

"It's what this camp is going to be all about." I take the chance and lay my hand on top of his, intertwining our fingers as we both feel our way around the sign. "You accepted me for who I am, and I want to give that same acceptance to kids of all ages. I want them to know it's more than okay to be themselves."

He turns to me and nods. "That's beautiful."

My heart does a little backflip of pleasure. It makes me all too enthusiastic as I continue. "Instead of weekly mass and ministry, we'll have a whole camp show and tell. That way kids can share what makes them special and unique. We'll have campers of every religion and every background here. I want it to be a place where everyone feels safe to be themselves."

"It sounds like a great place," he whispers, but he takes his hand away from mine and drops it at his side. There's still a wariness to him, a slight discomfort that he feels, and I hate that he's experiencing it with me.

"I understand why you don't want to be near me," I confess, swallowing harshly as I force myself to contain my emotions. "I just wanted you to see what you inspired."

He shakes his head with a scoff. "You have to stop changing things for me. How do you still not get it?"

But I do. I know what he's saying. I know that changing yourself for someone else ultimately won't lead you to happiness. I know change comes from within, and the biggest change is changing for you and you alone. "It's not all about you," I tease, trying to lighten the tension. "You just helped me figure out what I wanted."

"And what is it you want?" he asks, cocking his head as he examines me.

"I want to love who I am. I want to be able to be myself," I admit honestly. I take a step closer. "I want you."

He bites down on his bottom lip, his piercing wobbling as he trembles. He looks down at his boots. "I don't think I'm ready to forgive you."

"Baby, I'll ask for it every day if I have to because you are worth it," I say, tipping his chin up with my fingers. "You showed me that it was okay to be me. You brought excitement and thrill to my life when I needed it the most. Most importantly, you never turned your back on me even when you had a hundred reasons to do so."

"But…" His lips curl into a snarl that I try to soothe with my thumb. "But what about God?"

I drop my hand. Not because his comment stings but because this is the one thing I've struggled with the most. Although it's difficult to explain what I truly feel when it comes to God, I can tell him the honest truth. "I've been exploring other religions. Turns out, there are more than just Catholics out there. I'm not one hundred percent there, and I'm not saying that my insecurities have magically disappeared, but what I do believe is that God led me to you for a reason."

He grits his teeth. "It wasn't God—"

"Maybe not God. Maybe the universe. Maybe a magic squirrel in the sky who eats rainbows, I don't know. Whatever the case, I found you and you found me, and you changed my life for the better. I'm better now, Noah."

A single tear tracks down his cheek. "I want to believe that."

"I understand," I say solemnly, knowing that I can't erase all that's happened, all the damage I've caused him. "I asked you to try the first day here. If I can ask you just one more time, please consider trying."

He kicks the ground with his boot, rocking on his heels as he shoves his hands in his pockets. "I do need a place to stay for a bit."

"You're taking me back?" I ask, not bothering to hide the excitement in my voice.

"We're seeing where this goes," he states firmly. "I want to believe you're changing, but I can't go through this again."

"You won't have to. I'll prove it to you," I promise, threading my fingers through his hair, my fingers warm under his beanie. I sag with relief, dropping to my knees in front of him as I hug his middle. I bury my face in his stomach, and I can't hold back the tears. "I love you, Noah."

He tenses underneath me, and I think he's going to push me away. He doesn't. Instead, he pets the top of my head, lovingly stroking my hair as he lets out a deep breath. "I love you too, Jarred. So fucking much it hurts."

But I'll take away the pain. I'll make sure that he never has to feel it again. I'd move mountains and dry up rivers and catch the fucking moon for him.

Because he's mine and I'm his. No matter what.

CHAPTER 32
NOAH

I take a long deep drag of my joint, letting the high wash over me, relishing in the slight burn in my throat. I sit by the lake, sketchpad in hand, and try and replicate the smooth curve of the bank.

I've found myself a lot here in the past week, trying to settle my racing thoughts and my equally racing heart. Things have been... awkward between Jarred and me. It's not like we're ignoring each other—we are the only two people in the massive camp—but it's not like we've gone back to the way things were. We've been taking it slow, having every meal together before I disappear into my own bubble to work through my thoughts.

He's been amazingly patient with me, always with a wide smile on his face and love in his eyes. I want to give in so badly. I want to just say fuck it and forgive him, but something is holding me back. I think I'm just scared. Scared that this is only temporary, that all the changes he's made are superficial, that he'll turn on me again just like he did before.

So, I smoke. I get high and I sketch and I try to ignore all my problems like a well-adjusted adult should.

But I can't just make it all go away, not when I can hear Jarred trudging through the sand toward me. He sits down next to me, groaning as he does, and I resist the urge to smirk and tease him about his age. It feels too easy to fall back into old patterns. It feels too natural to remember our last interaction by the lake where he promised me the idea of a future.

"Hey, I was wondering where you went," he says. "What are you doing?"

"Drawing the lake," I say, not taking my eyes off my sketchpad. I'm liable to do something stupid like kiss that grin of his.

"Right," he mumbles, smacking his lips. "Can I have some of that?"

I can only assume he's talking about the joint dangling between my fingers. I give it to him without looking up. "Knock yourself out."

He hesitates for a second before taking it out of my hands. I can hear his deep inhale and smell the smoke as he blows it out in front of him. He leans in, breath heavy on the side of my neck, and I hear the wonder in his words. "Is that us?"

Fuck. I didn't even realize *that's* what I was drawing. I guess my subconscious is just too strong. I've drawn the lake, but I've focused on the spot hidden by the big boulder at the far end. I hadn't even real-ized I started drawing two figures in the water, their bodies close together, the tension palpable between them.

"It's the first thing that came to mind," I say, closing my sketchpad and tucking it away. I finally look up and my eyes zero in on the joint. "It's puff-puff-pass, old man."

He chuckles, and I smile at the sound. I just can't help myself. He hands me the joint, and it seems like his fingers want to linger on my skin, but I pull back before they can. He sighs but retains that sweet smile as he stares at me. "I know I've said it already, but I'm so glad you're here."

My heart constricts because deep inside me, I know my truth. I meet his brown gaze and raise the corner of my lip. "Yeah, me too."

"Have you looked into school yet?" he asks, calling back to when I mentioned it to him the other day, nervous about the prospect of doing it all on my own. "It's starting soon, right?"

"Yeah, just one more week," I say. "I still don't know how I'm going to do it without my parents' help."

I haven't spoken to them since they kicked me out. Fine. Good riddance. After processing what happened, I realized that I was better off without them and their outdated, poisonous influence. It's hard—they're my parents after all—but it's for the best.

"Maybe I can help you," he suggests, taking the joint from me after I've taken two hits.

I scoff. "I can't take your money."

"Good thing I don't have any money to give," he snorts. "I meant I could help you figure out some student loans. Maybe a payment plan?"

I'm grateful for that. I'll admit that I was privileged in the fact that my parents handled that for me before. Now I'm on my own, but I could still use the help.

You're not on your own...

"That would be cool," I say lamely, shaking that errant thought from my head. "I appreciate it."

"My laptop is in my cabin if you want to go now. Or if you want to keep drawing, that's fine too. We don't have to do it tonight. We can—"

I cut off his adorable babbling, smiling at the flush in his cheeks. He's really nervous around me, and I get it. I haven't really made things easy for him since I got here. But I soften because he's still the same Jarred with the same tics. Some things just don't change. "We can go now."

We both stand as I stub out the joint. I wish that we were walking hand in hand, but I don't think I'm ready for that yet. Although I enjoy the silence, I do want to try and make an effort, just like he is.

So, I start asking him questions ranging from how the reconstruction is going in the chapel to how he spent his morning. We talk about meaningless things, even though every piece of information fills my chest with something warm and fuzzy.

"What are you going to do now that camp is over?" I ask. I know he mentioned before that he sometimes planned events during the off-season, but I don't know if that's changed with the rebranding.

"I've been looking into seeing if the camp could partner with a nonprofit LGBTQIA+ organization. Maybe during the off-season, we can provide housing for the kids that have been kicked out or are on the streets." He shrugs, scratching the back of his blushing neck. "I guess the rest depends on you."

I furrow my brows. "How?"

"I was hoping I could go back to UNC with you." His eyes widen and he corrects himself. "I mean, we would get an apartment, and maybe you could stay with me on the weekends. I'd still drive up here, but we could have more time together."

I can't describe what it does to me that he's been seriously considering our future together. Before, he couldn't give me anything past *I don't know* and *for now*, but he's been thinking about it. It also makes me irrationally happy to think that he'd be willing to drive a total of twelve hours every week just to be close to me.

"That's very optimistic of you," I tease, knocking his shoulder with mine. He just chuckles lightly as we stand outside his cabin.

"I'd say more hopeful than anything." His expression turns serious, and he reaches for my hand. I give it to him, relishing in the way his calloused hand feels against my palm. "I really do love you, Noah. I want us to be together."

"Me too." I suck in a sharp breath. I can't believe tears are springing in my eyes. This is a good thing. It's a good thing that he's planning our future, that he's accepting me, and that he wants me. But... "It just...it still hurts."

His face softens as he tucks a stray hair behind my ear, his fingers gently tracing across my cheek to brush against the piercings in my nose. He leans down and kisses them both, resting his lips there for a second before pulling back. "I know, baby. I would take it away if I could. I'd turn back time and cut my own fucking tongue off."

I bite my bottom lip, fiddling with my piercing before I sigh. "I...I think I could move in with you. It would save me money. It's probably cheaper than paying for the dorms and the meal plan."

His brown eyes sparkle with joy as he cups my cheeks. "Yeah?"

"Yeah." I pull back, however, because there's still something that's not quite right. So, I change the subject as I open the cabin door and walk through. "So, how'd your first appointment with the therapist go?"

He mentioned that the other day, that he's started seeing a therapist to help him overcome the things that happened to him when he was younger. Apparently, Mary referred her to him the day he came back from visiting me. His therapist does virtual appointments, so it's been easy for him to incorporate it into his week.

"Good," he smiles as he heads to his kitchen table where his laptop rests. He speaks with his back to me as he starts up the computer. "Nothing was really solved, but we have a plan."

"That's great," I say, joining him at the table as I sit next to him. "I'm happy for you, Jarred."

His fingers still on the laptop as he turns to me. "I'm really trying, Noah."

"I know you are." I lean forward before I can stop myself, burying my head in his neck. The rapid beating of his pulse under my lips does something to me. I can't help but kiss the spot which makes him groan. "Jarred…"

"Give me a chance, baby," he whispers against the top of my head, wrapping his arms around me.

Can I do that? Can I give him one more piece of myself? Can I try to move on from everything he did and everything he said? Can I take the risk that my heart might break all over again someday?

It only takes his lips against my temple and his whispered confession of love to give me my answer.

Fuck yes.

He's changing. He's trying. He's moving on, and he wants to move on with me. He's shown me that he sees my worth. He's been patient with my process of trying to move past what happened.

He's a sweet soul—genuine and pure—and people make mistakes. I meant it when I said I would protect him, care for him, and be there for him. I'd be a hypocrite to turn my back on him now, especially when he's becoming his best self.

And, the most important part, is that he's doing it for himself.

He just wants me on the journey with him.

"Please," I whisper, brushing my lips gently against his as I let out a weak sob. "Please, don't hurt me again."

He lets out a muffled sob and drags me onto his lap. He cradles my face in his large hands, eyes penetrating my soul, all his intention and conviction as clear as the dusk sky. "Never. Never, baby. I'm yours and you're mine. No matter what."

And that's all it takes for me to smash my lips against his.

It feels like…it feels like the heaven I used to not believe in. It's the most glorious sensation—this passionate love-filled kiss—and it sparks a deep need inside me. Not just for his body but for *him*. It makes me feel like a fool for resisting him because I can taste his remorse and I can savor his promise and I can lick across the secret that we no longer are.

He lifts me effortlessly, bringing me blindly toward his bed, and laying me down gently across his comforter. His fingers rest on the hem of my shirt, and he waits for me to give him permission before raising it up and over my head. He then falls to his knees, going straight for my jeans and taking them off with accurate precision. I don't bother to hold back my satisfied moan when he takes me into his mouth, his tongue dancing around my dick piercing, his lips kissing every inch with wet and sloppy caresses.

When I can't take it anymore, when I need his naked body against mine, and when I yearn to be as close to him as possible, I gently tug on his hair to get his attention. "Babe…I want to make love to you."

He smiles against my hip, a devious smile on his lips as he kisses the spot that always makes me squirm. "I want that too."

"Get naked," I command, and he strips in such a rush that I have to laugh. He drapes his body on top of mine, and we both let out a relieved moan at the feeling of being together again like this.

He kisses my neck, licking and nipping at the skin. "Can I be on top? I want to show you how much I love you."

"Y—Yeah," I say, fumbling for the nightstand where I know he keeps the lube. I hand it to him, but he hesitates for a second. "What is it?"

For a second, I'm afraid his insecurities are going to rise up. I'm terrified that his shame and guilt are there, preventing him from going through with this. I feel like a fool, but he kisses me again and makes those thoughts disappear. He pulls back, sorrow in his eyes. "Do we… do we need a condom?"

I know what he's asking without needing to hear the words. I shake my head, wrapping my arms around his neck as I kiss him again. "No. There hasn't been anybody else."

"I wouldn't blame you—"

"Even if I wanted to, I couldn't. Not when it's always been you."

He nods against my forehead, a shaky and trembling smile on his lips. He turns around and presents that glorious ass to me, handing me the lube so I can slick up my fingers. I ease into him slowly, tenderly, giving him time to adjust to one finger, two fingers, and then three.

"I'm ready," he says, turning around so he's facing me. He takes the lube from me and coats my cock in it, throwing the bottle to the side as he positions my cock at his puckered entrance. He rubs it against his hole teasingly, and it's agony.

"Don't make me take control," I threaten, lightly spanking his ass to get him moving. When he wantonly moans, incoherent and so fucking filthy, I put that in my memory bank for later.

He puts me out of my misery as he slides down my length, and we both shudder when his ass meets my hips. He stills for a moment, running his hands up and down my chest with reverence. "You're so beautiful, Noah."

"You too, babe," I say, and fuck I never knew I could cry this much in my life. "Go ahead. Love me."

He leans down to peck my lips. "There was never a choice."

He rocks his hips back and forth, driving out long groans from me as he whimpers in pleasure. He looks incredible like this—confident, shameless, indulgent—and it only reaffirms my decision to give him this chance. He's showing me with his body that he's come to accept who he is. He's demonstrating with every ghost of a touch that I'm his and he's mine.

No matter what.

When his breath hitches and his hips slam down against me, I smirk. "You going to come for me, babe? You want me to fill that ass with my cum until you're leaking?"

He throws his head back, nails digging into my skin as he nods dumbly. "Yes...yes...Noah...*more!*"

I know exactly what he's asking for. He loves it when I talk dirty to him. He takes every single filthy thing I say and lets it fuel his eventual release. I'll give it to him. I'll give him everything.

My hands latch onto his hips as I help his motions. "We have so much time to make up for. How should we spend it? Fucking you in every inch of this camp?"

"Yes!"

"You should always have that ass prepped and ready for me, so I can slide in and take my man whenever I want him."

"*Please!*"

"You're going to be at my beck and call, babe. You're going to be so fucking sore, but you'll beg."

"I'm gonna...I'm gonna..."

I still his movements. "Not until you get a finger up my ass and fuck me with it."

He's so quick to comply. He scrambles to the other side of the bed, somehow managing to keep me inside him. His wet fingers are on my ass not a second later, driving into me as he keeps fucking me. I love it. I love how we could be so sweet and tender and then become dirty as fuck.

Because I love him. I love everything about him. I fell in love with the whispered secrets and now I love the screeching truth even more.

"Fuck me, I'm going to cum," I grunt. I take his cock in my hand, jacking him roughly just how he likes it. "Come for me, Jarred. You've been so good for me. Get your reward."

He comes with my name screamed from his lips. I finish right after him, holding his body tight against mine as he collapses in my arms. I kiss his sweaty forehead, brushing his hair away from his face as I look down at him.

"We're...we're getting there, aren't we?" he asks, and I have to chuckle because I remember when he spoke those same words to me weeks ago.

"Yeah," I mumble against his puffy lips, nipping at his jaw as I descend to his neck. "We are."

We're going to get there. We're going to move past this. We're going to be together—out loud and free—and this long painful journey will have been worth it.

"We have the rest of our lives to," he adds, resting his cheek against my pec. "I really fucking love you, Noah Scott."

"And I really fucking love you, Jarred Walker."

With my entire angry, bitter, vulnerable, sometimes sweet, heart.

EPILOGUE

One Year Later

I still love the first day of camp.

As I look around at all the bubbly campers, I smile with pride. It took work to get this many people to sign up. We had to promote the crap out of this place, even diving into social media which Noah had to painstakingly talk me through. It's still not as many campers as I used to get but that's okay. I have a different mission now, and I'll be happy to simply spread it to as many people as I can. Kids of all ages—seven to seventeen—all tumble in. I'm surprised to see that some of these campers are returners. It seems that some parents could forgive and understand the fucked-up situation that happened last year.

What's even more surprising is that most of my counselors are also returners. It makes my chest beam with respect and admiration for them. Kendall and Patrick are here, having been loyal and steadfast in this journey to a new beginning. I've given them more responsibilities at camp, making sure they know just how much I appreciate everything they've done to help me.

My twins stand by the entrance, happily chatting away with some campers. My heart swells at seeing them here. Even though Jenny signed the divorce papers a few months ago, the twins still spend as much time as they can with me.

Not surprisingly in the least, all of the counselors let out a breath of relief at the fact that Bryce wasn't coming back. Apparently, I had been blind all these years to what a monster that kid really is. We pressed charges against him for what he did, but they got dismissed, giving him only community service for his crime. Although Noah still swears he'll kill him if he ever sees him again, I've taken a more righteous path. I've forgiven him just like God would want.

God.

I feel him every day. His warmth, his love, his guidance. It's comforting now, not stifling, to believe in a God that believes in *me.*

"You nervous?"

I smile as I turn to my incredible boyfriend. Noah's wearing his new Camp Acceptance polo, clipboard in hand as he surveys the campers. He wanted to be a part of this process as much as I wanted him to be. I'm grateful for the fact that this past year, he'd drive up with me sometimes during the weekend to help me get everything set up. UNC has been great to him, providing him with a combination of loans and scholarships to get him through the rest of college.

"I'm excited," I say, rubbing his back tenderly as he fusses with the list in his hand. I lean down and whisper in his ear. "I think I should get a congratulatory treat later for getting all this done."

He scoffs but leans into my touch. "I think *I* deserve a treat. You know how much shit you put me in charge of? How did you manage to do this on your own?"

"You have Father Matteo to help you," I chuckle, gesturing at our resident priest. He's not going to be leading mass but, instead, he's going to be in charge of the multi-spiritual center we converted the chapel into. "You're just too stubborn to ask for help."

He scoffs. "As if I need the help." His eyes widen as he circles something on the list. "Fuck, maybe I do. I forgot all about welcome packets! Fuck!"

"It'll be okay, baby," I say with ease, not stressing in the slightest. "Why don't you go see to that before you stress out even more."

"Right," he says with a curt nod of his head. Absentmindedly, and just like our routine, he leans up on his toes to press a quick kiss to my lips. Just like that. In public where I happily accept. "My old-ass boyfriend is so wise."

I playfully knock my shoulder into his. "Go, you little shit."

He laughs and kisses me once again before rushing to Kendall who also seems panicked about the welcome packets. I take a moment to bask in it all.

Noah and I are okay. We've made it work. I've come a long way from where I was a year ago—alone and scared—not embracing who I truly am. Now, Noah and I are happily together, not hiding, not coated in shame, no longer secrets whispered in the dusk. We're *real*.

I pat at the little box in my pocket, chuckling to myself as I picture the look on his face when I show it to him tonight at a dinner I planned by the lake.

What Noah doesn't know is that by the end of this night, he'll no longer refer to me as his boyfriend, but his fiancé.

BONUS EPILOGUE

Want to see the sweet and smutty proposal? Join my newsletter to see Jarred and Noah's happily ever after!

Subscribe and read!

WHAT COMES NEXT

Say hello to *Their Ball Boy*! Fun, sporty...and MMM!

Coming Feb 6th!

Preorder Here!

Blurb:

Bryson

I'm a walking disaster.

I'm awkward, perpetually uncomfortable, and afraid of everything. Truly an example of natural selection at its worst.

After a series of dead-end jobs, I'm now working with my disappointed dad as a ball boy for his team of superstars. It's the only thing I've got going for me, even if I know it's only a matter of time before I fail epically.

Then I meet them.

World-famous soccer players Dalton Cross and Juandi Fernandez couldn't be any more different. While one relishes control in all aspects of his life, the other takes everything day by day. They're polar opposites, always butting heads, and always trying to one-up the other.

Somehow they both want me.

Dalton makes me feel safe, protected, and cherished—something no one's ever cared to do before. Juandi makes me feel wild, free, and courageous—something that was sorely lacking in my sheltered life.

Being with them is a dream I never thought possible for someone like me, but the secrets we buried are surfacing, and I'm worried about what this means for our future together. I've never been the main character—never been the chosen one.

But this time, I'm willing to do whatever it takes to hold on to the two things I can't afford to lose.

Their Ball Boy is an insta-attraction, super steamy MMM romance with one bumbling ball boy, two world-famous soccer players, and the spiciness that occurs between the three. Mingle in a grumpy/sunshine trope, first-times, plenty of kinks, and you're in for a while ride. CWs include but are not limited to mental health representation, emotionally distant parents, and mild daddy kink (no age play). For a full breakdown of TWs and CWs, please visit www. addisonbeckromance.com

ACKNOWLEDGMENTS

As usual, I would like to take the time to thank everyone who was involved with this.

To my amazing PA—Mads at Breathless Lit—you have been amazing and inspiring. You've helped me through every step and made me remember that my words have value. Thank you for being the best PA, friend, and cheerleader a writer can have.

Colleen, Emma, Nerida, Francesca, Nicole, and A.E. Jensen: You were all wonderful betas whose amazingness helped this story come to life.

Cora—sweet, kind, funny Cora—thank you for inspiring one particularly spicy scene. Thanks for not letting me get *caged* in (see what I did there)?

Corinne C. Rochelle: Thank you for your awesome blurb-age skills and for helping me sort out the words when I didn't know how to get them out.

ABOUT THE AUTHOR

Thanks for reading. I'm Addison Beck and I love all things sweet, smutty, and sinful. I'm a bit of an awkward turtle that can be found in her little shell eating sushi and binging horror movies with my two cats.

Stalk much?

- Join my newsletter to get ALL the updates!
- Subscribe to my Patreon for all the goodies including NSFW art and never-before-seen content!
- Be a part of my Facebook Group where my crazy thoughts are shared!
- Follow me on Instagram and tag me in your reviews or posts!

ALSO BY ADDISON BECK